“My Sources Say You Paid Cash For This Building. Where Did You Get That Kind Of Money, Miss Raines?”

Sources? She considered him again. Finely chiseled nose and brow, a perfectly square, utterly masculine jaw. Dark eyes with lush lashes. And his mouth… His lips might be full and soft in the rare moments he wasn’t scowling. But none of that really mattered now. No, what mattered was drawing a line of acceptable behavior and then holding it.

“Mr. Preston, my personal finances are none of your business.”

“I can find out,” he countered.

“Well, you just put your pet ferret right on that,” she challenged. “Do let me know wh
I’m sure it’ll be fascir

He gave her a long, h
certain of it.”

Dear Reader,

It has been such a treat to work on the GIFTS FROM A BILLIONAIRE series. An intriguing premise, the chance to collaborate with creative friends, and an editor who trusts our visions and voices…it's the stuff of a writer's dreams.

And the stuff of dreams is precisely what this series is all about. Take one good person trying to make the world a better place, add an unexpected gift from an anonymous donor, and then stir in the sweet tumult of finding the love of their lives along the way…. Ah, how wonderful life can truly be.

It's my pleasure to present you with *The Money Man's Seduction,* the second story in this series. I sincerely hope you enjoy the story of Emily Raines, a nationally renowned artist and crusader for elder services, and Cole Preston, a successful venture capitalist who firmly believes that most social angels are really scam artists in disguise. The dreamer and the cynic. The do-gooder and the money man.

They say that opposites attract. Or is it really more a case of two open hearts finding common ground in the pursuit of what really matters in life?

I'll let you read Emily and Cole's story and decide for yourself. Happy reading!

Leslie LaFoy

THE MONEY MAN'S SEDUCTION

LESLIE LaFOY

Silhouette® Desire

Published by Silhouette Books
America's Publisher of Contemporary Romance

ISBN-13: 978-0-373-76898-1
ISBN-10: 0-373-76898-2

THE MONEY MAN'S SEDUCTION

This edition published by arrangement with Harlequin Books S.A.

Visit Silhouette Books at www.eHarlequin.com

Printed in U.S.A.

Books by Leslie LaFoy

Silhouette Desire

The Money Man's Seduction #1898

Silhouette Special Edition

Blindsided #1716

Harlequin Next

Grin and Bear It

LESLIE LAFOY

lives in a small town on the Kansas prairie with her husband, two dogs and four cats. With a bachelor's degree in the administration of justice and a master's in sociology (criminology), Leslie serves as the unofficial poster child of overeducation. Having taught high school social studies for fifteen years, she turned her creative energies to writing historical romances and the rest is, as they say, history.

Between her sixteenth and seventeenth published book, Leslie and her husband bought two commercial buildings on the National Historic Register and committed the rest of their lives and all their fortunes to restoring them to their 1884 glory.

When not up to her chin in sawdust, plaster and paint, Leslie writes books, serves on the City Council and the board of the local Main Street Association, and sends care packages to her son who serves his country in the United States Navy.

You can contact Leslie at her Web site, www.leslielafoy.com.

For Mary, Joan and Kasey,
friends and fellow storysmiths.

And for MJ,
the best and most patient editor in the world.

Prologue

Well, my darling devotees, it's just a few months into the RBGS—that's Reclusive Billionaire Giving Season for those of you who have only recently joined the ranks of Inquiring Minds. Taking most seriously my responsibilities as your trusted purveyor of vital information, I assure you that I have had my ear constantly tuned to hear even the slightest whisper of rumor and speculation about who this year's lucky largesse recipients might be.

And while the tidbits are absolutely stunning, my dear fans, I'm not quite yet prepared to let the names of this crop of golden kitties out of Santa's bag. But for those of you who have been inspired by *moi* to collect tidbits on your own… Well, darling, call me; we'll do lunch and compare our notes. Reporting most definitely has its rewards, you know.

Sam Balfour placed the newspaper clipping on the desktop. "Have you seen this? The last item." He didn't wait for a response. "I warned you this barracuda isn't going to let you alone. She doesn't know anything concrete yet, or at least I hope she doesn't. Otherwise she wouldn't be trolling her readership to get names. Hell, I should call her myself. Then maybe you'll realize that it's time to stop this crazy game."

S. Edward Balfour IV, known to his nephew as Uncle Ned, only smiled as he trumped Sam's newspaper with the dark green manila folder he removed from the top desk drawer. "Deal with this, please, before you rush out to call the woman and set a date for your luncheon rendezvous."

Sam sighed as he looked at the folder. Green, for giving. How many more folders just like it did Uncle Ned have sitting in that drawer? "I talk, but you don't listen. I'm only trying to protect you, you know."

"And I appreciate your love and concern," Ned told him. "That does not, however, mean I'm ready to abandon Maureen's project. Please see that the usual funds are delivered within the week."

Sam only glanced at the Letter to the Editor his uncle had circled before checking the top of the page and the name of the newspaper. "You keep having to cast your net wider and wider to find candidates, don't you? I never heard of this place. Is it even on the map?"

"I could send you instead of Bruce, and then you could find out for yourself."

"And be more involved in your project than I am now? Thanks, but I'd rather have a root canal," Sam said, and gave up the argument. Santa Ned wasn't going to be convinced. At least not yet. He closed the folder and tucked it under his arm. "I'll have Bruce take the company jet."

"Bruce is a good man. Very discreet."

"Three cheers for Bruce." Sam was about to turn and leave his uncle's office, but then hesitated. "You know what, Uncle Ned? I don't know if I should be hoping this Emily Raines is a good pick or a bad one. I don't know which result would be better for you."

"You think too much, Sam. Better you should learn how to feel. True joy is in the giving, not what happens once that gift is given. Anything beyond the giving is out of our hands."

One

There were no half-naked nymphets scattering flower petals and the red Porsche wasn't exactly a classic chariot, but the man getting out of it was a certified Greek god. Emily Raines rested her forearms on the handle of the still-unplugged industrial floor sander and watched the stranger through the front window. Tall, broad shoulders, narrow hips and dark hair just long enough to blow in the light breeze. The easy way he moved as he reached back inside the car for his suit jacket….

Emily smiled appreciatively and wondered if he had his pants tailored so that they pulled extra nicely over his gym-honed muscles when he bent over. Lord Almighty, if he was here in Augsburg, Kansas, taking nymphet applications, she just might be tempted to fill one out.

"Emily!"

Half her brain recognized her friend's arrival from somewhere in the old building. The other half went on with a fantasy of see-through togas, reclining sofas and grapes.

"I'm telling you," Beth declared, "this whole deal is a bona fide case of no good deed going unpunished."

Ah, he was looking up and down the street. Maybe he was lost. "You are such a pessimist. Such a CPA." Maybe she should be a nice person and wander out to see if he needed directions.

"Realist," Beth countered, waving a handful of papers. "Estimates tend to do that for most people. Fifteen thousand or fifteen-five for a new roof. Your choice."

"Which roofer looked more interested in doing it?" she asked as Mr. Adonis's attention came to her building…and stayed. Her heart added a happy little beat in anticipation.

"Quite frankly, they both looked like they'd rather take a beating."

Okay, he was crossing the street. She had just enough time to do a setup. "Speaking of contractor beatings," she said, quickly turning to Beth. "Would you go back and talk to the electrician until I can get there?" She nodded toward the street. "It looks like we're going to have a visitor."

Beth glanced toward the glass front doors, arched an auburn brow, tucked a fiery red curl behind her ear and grinned. "Scream if you need help," she offered, laughing and heading for the door at the back of the office. "Loud if you're serious about it. It's a big building."

Need help? Ha! Emily glanced back toward the front just long enough to gauge her timing, and then began to ever-so-casually unwind the cord of the sander. The bell over the door jangled. Emily put what she hoped looked like a serene-but-pleasantly-semi-surprised smile on her face and looked up.

"Hello," Adonis said.

Oh, be still her heart. A voice that rumbled, deep and slow and low. "Hi," she vaguely heard herself reply as she watched his gaze slide slowly down to openly marvel over the fact that she'd bought her T-shirt in Jackson Hole. It moved lower still to the frayed edges of her cutoff jeans and right on down, smooth as silk, to the tops of her leather work boots. It returned upward—every bit as appreciatively—to finally meet her own.

He smiled, lopsidedly, the light in his eyes a delicious combination of guilt and pleasure.

Emily reined in her own smile and managed to tamp the more obvious notes of hope out of her voice as she asked, "What can I do for you?"

The guilt part evaporated out of his smile and his eyes sparkled with clear understanding. "I'm Cole Preston and I'm wondering if you've seen my grandmother this morning. She said she was coming here. Ida Bentley?"

Well, this was even better. Hardly a stranger at all. Emily grinned. "Ida's an absolute sweetheart. A truly incredible woman."

Sadness replaced the easy pleasure in his smile as he nodded. "She's also got a few screws that aren't quite as tight as they used to be. And I have the checkbook to prove it."

"Well, yes," Emily allowed diplomatically as her stomach fluttered and went a little cold. "I have noticed that Ida's mind tends to drift a bit every now and then."

"More than a bit," he countered. "And every now and then is more like often."

"I think she maintains very well for an eighty-something-year-old woman," Emily offered brightly in her elderly friend's defense. "Ida is always dressed not only impeccably, but also perfectly appropriately for the weather and the occasion. And she's gracious, delightful company. She's been coming in every day since we started working on the building and she has some wonderful ideas for classes once we're up and running."

"That would be the classes on modern interpretive dance." Cool, distant, definitely disapproving.

"Well, of course," Emily answered. "Your grandmother was a professional dancer. Judging by the scrapbooks she's shown us, she was very highly regarded in her time."

"That was then. This is now. Her time is over."

Over? "I beg your pardon?" she asked as in her mind's eye she saw Ida huddled on an iceberg being shoved out to sea.

"People need to stop filling my grandmother's head with the idea that she can still dance."

So much for the hope of Mr. Wonderful wandering in off the street. The man certainly looked like the stuff of feminine dreams, but the nice suit and the well-toned body only disguised the fact that he had all the emotional sensitivity of…of…well, she'd think of something really cold and heartless later.

At the moment, all she could really think about was how pathetically desperate she was. To think she'd been willing to drop her toga and share her grapes with him. Shaking her head and silently mourning the untimely—and not to mention brutally quick—death of the most inspiring fantasy she'd had in years, Emily plugged the cord of the sander into the wall socket.

"We obviously disagree on your grandmother's capabilities," she countered with a shrug. "It's clear, though, that she's a considerably kinder and less judgmental person than her grandson."

He blinked and opened his mouth to speak, but she didn't give him a chance to actually spit any words out. "I haven't seen Ida this morning, Mr. Preston. She could be over at the café or the gift shop. You might check there."

"Well, maybe it's a good thing she isn't here yet," he said, either missing the fact that he'd been dismissed, or choosing to ignore it. Neither possibility counted in his favor. "It'll give me a chance to take care of business."

Business? She wasn't a business. She was a nonprofit community organization for the elderly. The rural elderly. Or would be once she got the place fixed up. Not that she needed to tell him any of that. Holding the handles of the floor sander in the classic I'm-busy-let's-get-this-over-with pose, she met his gaze again. Or tried to, anyway. His gaze was taking another Fantastic Voyage to her boot laces and back. Since his attention was otherwise engaged…

Emily considered the long length of his lean legs, the broad width of his chest, the way the dark hair at his nape brushed against the crisp white of his shirt collar. She arched a brow.

Maybe she'd been too quick to give up the torrid affair thing. It wasn't as though she was looking for Prince Charming and the whole forever-in-a-happy-castle deal. Cole Preston was sculpted, hot, and no doubt about it, interested. It would be a real shame to waste such an incredible opportunity.

And not just a shame, either. It could very well be a crime. Like leaving a perfectly fitting pair of jeans in the store dressing room was a crime against the shopping gods. Wonderful things were put in your path for a reason and you took a big chance if you didn't properly appreciate them. And gosh, she certainly didn't want to risk offending the gods of a breathless good time.

She softly cleared her throat. "What kind of business do you need to conduct, Mr. Preston?"

"Do you know if an Emily Raines person is here?"

An Emily Raines person. Well, as Ida would say, how perfectly ill-mannered. The man just couldn't seem to stop digging a hole for himself.

"I'm Emily Raines," she said crisply.

He not only blinked, but actually rocked back a little on the heels of his finely made Italian leather shoes. Emily didn't give him a chance to regain his balance. "You said that you had something you wanted to talk with me about, Mr. Preston. What is it? I have a electrician waiting out back to tell me how much of the Earth it's going to cost to bring this building into the twentieth century."

"In case you haven't noticed," he replied, offering her a smile that looked decidedly strained, "it's the twenty-first century."

Emily sweetly replied, "Actually, I have noticed that, Mr. Preston. But I can't afford to wire this place for the latest bells and whistles. The tail end of the last century will have to be good enough for now."

He looked up at the rusty spots in the tin ceiling tiles. "And where are you planning to get the money for electricians?"

Her shock lasted only a nanosecond. Anger took over after that. Propping her hip against the built-in antique desk and crossing her arms over her midriff, she coolly replied, "The etiquette lessons are being held over at the high school."

His brows knitted for a moment before he quietly cleared his throat and asked, "Excuse me?"

"I said that the etiquette lessons are being held over at the high school. The class is designed for the teenage girls in town," she went on, embellishing the bold-faced lie. "But I'm sure that given your very obvious need for them, they'll let you participate."

His dark eyes sparked and the muscles in his jaw pulsed.

"The class started just a few minutes ago," she added.

"If you hurry, you won't have missed much. I'm sure there will be a section on how it's considered grossly impolite to ask total strangers about the details of their personal finances."

"Will there be a section," he asked smoothly, "on how it's illegal to bilk senile little old ladies out of their social security checks?"

As accusations went, that one hadn't even been thinly veiled, but she wasn't about to launch into a spirited self-defense. That would imply a guilty conscience. And since she didn't have a damn thing to feel even the least bit guilty about, she wasn't going to give him the satisfaction of so easily putting her on the defensive. No, she was going to make him say it straight out.

"Who do you think is bilking whom, Mr. Preston?"

"I suspect that you are bilking—or at least attempting to—my grandmother."

Emily silently counted to five before she allowed herself to ask, "And what, exactly, leads you to think this?"

"My grandmother thinks supporting this...this..." He glanced around the old office, cocking one eyebrow and looking decidedly less than visionary.

"The building itself used to be a produce warehouse," Emily explained. "I'm in the process of turning it into a fine arts center for senior citizens. And you should know that I haven't taken so much as a single solitary cent from—"

"And if I have my say in it, you're not going to, either."

She had to count to six this time. "Look," Emily said tightly, her pulse pounding furiously, "let's get something straight, Mr. Preston. Your grandmother hasn't said a word to me about donating anything other than her time and considerable artistic talents once we're up and running. If she were to offer me money, I'd turn her down. This—"

He made a sound that was part sigh, part snort.

If the sander hadn't weighed a ton and a half, she'd have snatched it up and beaten him with it. "Do you make it a habit to go around insulting the ethics and integrity of everyone you meet?"

"Just those I think are attempting to take advantage of my grandmother's failing mind."

Clearly there was no reasoning with the man. He was going to believe what he wanted to believe and neither the facts nor any assertions from her were going to make the least bit of difference to his thinking. And given that unfortunate reality, there wasn't any point in pulling her punches. "You have to be the most insuf—"

The door bell jangled and Emily instantly snapped her mouth closed. She was just giving him a try-to-be-civil-for-two-seconds look when a familiar voice said brightly and cheerfully, "Oh, I was hoping you two would get to meet today."

"Yes, we've just met, Ida," Emily replied as Cole Preston smiled and planted a kiss on the cheek of his elegantly slim, silver-haired grandmother. Emily added, "Although, I really gotta say that I can't imagine why you'd want us to."

Ida chuckled softly and patted his arm. "Cole's all

bark and no bite, dear. If I don't want to go to one of those retirement villages, I'm not going. He can stamp his feet and gnash his teeth all he wants. It's not going to make any difference."

Retirement home? Again Emily's mind put the all the pieces together in a single second. Inching her way into what—by her quick count—was the third round of her and Cole Preston's "How Many Ways Can I Dislike You?" game, she asked, "Are we talking about an assisted living facility?"

"Yes," he answered with a crisp, brief nod. "She would be better off there."

"Really?" Emily answered, accepting his challenge. "Says who? You?"

Ida chuckled again. "Give him hell, Emily. Is Beth around somewhere?" She patted her Gucci handbag. "I brought her some of that jojoba oil I got out in Santa Fe last year."

How such a sweet and generous person could be related to such a pompous… "She's back in the rear section talking with the electrician," Emily supplied, squarely meeting Cole Preston's self-assured gaze.

Ida nodded and walked off toward the rear office door, saying as she went, "Cole, help Emily, please. That machine, whatever it's for, is much too big for her to handle all by herself."

He didn't move. And despite the fact that he didn't look as though he had any intention of doing so, Emily wanted to be sure. "Touch it and die."

"I wouldn't lift a finger to help you," he replied. "I

don't want to be considered even a minor accessory when you're hauled off on fraud charges."

"Yeah, defending yourself would really distract you from your efforts to get your grandmother locked up nice and tight in some veggie bin."

Both brows went up. "Veggie bin?" he repeated as the corner of his mouth twitched upward and the cool distance in his eyes turned into a sparkle of amusement.

Her pulse skittering and her heart fluttering, Emily glared down at the floor and collected what she could of her suddenly scattered outrage. God, she couldn't even remember what she'd said that had triggered the unnerving change in him. And her. Damn. Round One had been about his belief that the elderly shouldn't do anything more physically strenuous than sit in a rocker and drool the day away. Round Two had been his baseless assumption that she was a con artist preying on the elderly. Round Three had started with the mention of Ida being put in a home. Ah, now she remembered where she'd been going!

"Are you the only grandchild?" Emily asked bluntly.

His amusement was gone in a heartbeat. "I'm Ida's only living relative," he responded, his tone cool again, but this time with a slightly wary edge to it. "It's my responsibility to see that she's cared for and that she doesn't do anything physically dangerous or financially unwise."

"By financially unwise you mean write checks to questionable charitable causes like..." Emily paused to look around her for the dramatic effect of it. "Oh, just for the sake of an example, let's say a senior citizen fine arts center."

"You would be just one and the latest among many of the questionable hands stuck out, looking for a sizable donation from her."

Since the man just didn't have any bounds at all... "Well, I can certainly understand your perspective on the matter," Emily drawled. "What she gives to charity would probably come out of your inheritance."

"I don't need her money," he countered, sounding truly offended. "I happen to be very well-off financially."

"Or so you say," she allowed with a shrug, pleased with having so easily pushed his buttons. Fair was fair, after all; he'd certainly been pushing all of hers. "Then again, the Porsche could be a rental and you could have picked up the Brooks Brothers suit and the fancy Italian shoes at a Goodwill store in an upscale part of town. You never know. Appearances can be deceiving."

"In my case, I can assure you that appearances are reality."

Big Woo. As if she cared. "Would it come as a great shock to you to learn that maybe you aren't the only person in this room who's financially secure?"

He laughed, the sound striking her as way more condescending than amused. "Nice try, Miss Raines. You get points for attempting the bluff. Aside from the fact that it was a poorly executed effort, I've had you investigated and—"

"Investigated?" Oh, the low-life son of a—

"The first time my grandmother mentioned this…" He looked around the office again.

"Fine…arts…center," Emily supplied slowly, crisply. "Three words, Mr. Preston. A total of four whole syllables. Let's try to remember them."

"I had my assistant do some checking on you."

"Oh?" *Couldn't be bothered with doing it yourself?* "And what interesting tidbits did your personal ferret find?"

"You're relatively well-known in the historic preservation community for your stained glass repair work."

She decided not to mention that there was no "relatively" about her professional reputation; he'd probably never heard of the Smithsonian Institution. The impressive fact that she was in their go-to contact file would be completely lost on him.

"And, of course," Emily said with a tight smile of frayed patience, "me being well-regarded professionally led you to immediately suspect me of being a scam artist who specializes in fleecing the unsuspecting elderly. Yeah, I can see how you came to that conclusion. Pure logic at its best."

He shrugged. "You make a decent enough living for an artist type."

"An artist type. Boy, are you racking up the points. Do you refer to your grandmother as an artist type?"

For a second the corners of his mouth tightened. "But your credit rating suggests," he said, plowing ahead, undeterred, "that you don't make enough with your glass chips to qualify for a bank loan to buy a building like this. At least not a loan with a reputable bank."

There was so much fodder for offense in that statement that she could go off in ten different directions for a week, but if he wasn't going to be sidetracked, she wasn't either. "Isn't someone's personal credit information considered confidential?"

"Except to industry insiders," he replied offhandedly. "My sources say you paid cash for this building. Where did you get that kind of money, Miss Raines?"

Insiders? Sources? She considered him again. Finely chiseled nose and brow, a perfectly square, utterly masculine jaw. Dark eyes with lush lashes. And his mouth... His lips might be full and soft in the rare moments he wasn't scowling. All in all, he sort of reminded her of Hugh Jackman. Yeah, he was definitely handsome. Too bad he was way too abrasive to pull off a successful information schmooze. But none of that really mattered at the moment. No, what mattered was drawing a line of acceptable behavior and holding it.

"Forgive my bluntness, Mr. Preston, but Ida's grandson or God's grandson, insider or outsider of whatever industry—I really don't care. My personal finances are none of your business."

"I can find out," he countered.

"Well, you just put your pet ferret right on that," she challenged, wondering what law he was violating and what it would take to get him charged. "Do let me know what he turns up. I'm sure it'll be fascinating stuff."

"I'm absolutely certain of it. I'll bet it's a very long list of names like Edna and Ralph and Ida."

Hell, she'd take any name. Not that she was going to tell Cole Preston that. She'd been calling her anonymous benefactor "Secret Santa" for the last three weeks and while it worked in a casual way, she wanted to have a real name and an address to go with it so that she could write a proper thank-you note. Without Santa and the cashier's check for fifty grand, the center would still be nothing more than a dream.

"Like I said," she retorted as she pushed off the old desk and reached for the handles of the sander, "go for it. Now, if you'll excuse me, I have work to do."

She paused, smiled at him and added, "The first rule of running a successful con is to look like you don't need anyone's money, you know. I'm figuring that refinished oak floors ought to be enough to lull Mrs. Flores into giving me her weekly bingo money. And if I can get two or three other old ladies to do the same… Look out, Vegas, here I come."

"Sarcasm—"

Emily flipped the switch on the handle and the motor on the sander roared to life. His next few words were drowned out by the clatter of the accelerating blades. Whatever else he might have been intending to say was swallowed as the blades bit into the floor with more force than Emily had anticipated and the machine lurched forward out of her control.

While Emily tightened her grip and dug in her heels in a desperate effort to gain control of the wildly surging monster, Cole Preston displayed a keen sense of self-preservation and jumped out of the way.

The machine was making a slow left turn with Emily fighting it every inch of the way, when he stepped to her side and flipped off the power switch. The motor stopped instantly.

"You're a menace," he declared as the blades clattered to silence.

Her hands white on the handles and her cheeks hot with embarrassment and anger, Emily retorted, "Better than being a pathetic excuse for a grandson."

He glared at her in silence. Emily glared back and, not suffering from any sudden onset of muteness, added, "Kindly haul your sorry ass out of my *fine... arts...center.*"

His jaw clenched and his pulse clearly pounding in his temples, he turned on his heel and strode out of the building without another word. Emily watched him go, hating herself for having noticed that he wore a really yummy aftershave. A deep and dark spice with woodsy notes and just a hint of some sort of flower. She sighed and shook her head to dispel the ridiculous preoccupation.

At least, Emily consoled herself as she left the office in search of Ida, Beth and the electrician, she'd delivered a fabulous last line. The "sorry ass" part of it had been pure inspiration. Not the least bit physically accurate, of course, but...

She smiled, imagining him frantically checking out his butt in the first mirror he came across. Yeah, it was a shallow and probably fleeting triumph, but she'd take it. She had a niggling suspicion that in a contest of wills with Cole Preston, even the smallest of victories counted.

Two

Cole Preston walked down the sidewalk beside his grandmother, telling himself that he'd had worse days. Lots of them. Not that he could recall any of them at this particular moment. In looking back at the day so far… No, actually his world had gone off the rails yesterday afternoon when Grams had called him wanting—out of the absolute clear blue sky—to liquidate part of her investment portfolio so she could give it to a new friend of hers who was doing wonderful charity work.

The alarm bells had gone off in his head. Two hours later Wendy had been furious with him for canceling their date to the symphony—again—and he was heading for the middle of nowhere to do his family duty.

Six lanes of bumper-to-bumper Kansas City rush-hour traffic and then dodging pot holes on eighty miles of narrow two-lane road later, he'd arrived to find his grandmother with a heating pad in the small of her back, popping ibuprofen like candy and gushing over darling Emily Raines and the chance to dance again.

Darling? *Darling?* Yeah, okay, he'd allow that Emily Raines was drop-dead gorgeous. Legs from here to eternity, luscious curves in all the right places, and he couldn't remember the last time he'd seen a T-shirt stretched so invitingly over what looked like a perfect set of breasts. Add in a smile that lit up a room, curly blond hair, a perky little nose and a chin that she could square in the blink of her incredibly green eyes. No doubt about it, his Grams's new friend was a knockout.

But she was no darling by any stretch of even the most creative imagination. He'd been ten miles outside of town yesterday when Jason had called with the information from the first run of the background software. An artist who, until the last year, hadn't lived anywhere in her adult life longer than six months, a woman who suddenly showed up in a little bitty town with a wad of cash to buy a rundown building and saying she wanted to make life better for the elderly. It met the classic definition of suspicious.

Not that anyone but he and Jason thought so. Grams was absolutely convinced that her precious Emily was nothing short of an angel, an angel sent by the God of Days of Faded Glory Returned. Yeah, right. How anyone with such a quick temper and a sharp tongue could be considered angelic was beyond him. An angel from hell, maybe.

But since Grams didn't see Emily the same way he did, he was in one helluva bind. His original plan to blow into town, lay down the law, make arrangements for Grams to move to a more protected environment and blow out again obviously wasn't going to cut it.

And that first meeting with Emily Raines… He hadn't mangled a face-to-face with a woman that badly since junior high. He'd been pacing the living room of his grandmother's house desperately trying to come up with a workable plan B when she'd come home to chew him up one side and down the other for the way he'd behaved toward her Little Miss Perfect. She'd concluded the verbal lashing with the demand that he be nice to Emily, even if he had to fake it.

And in that moment, he'd found his solution. There was a saying about keeping your friends close and your enemies closer. If ever there was a situation when that advice applied, it was this one. So what if Grams thought he was a cross between a choirboy and a Boy Scout for saying that he would apologize to Emily Raines? It was the end result that mattered. And the odds of Emily Raines being able to commit mischief, mayhem and criminal fraud would be considerably lessened if he could keep her in his hip pocket. While being perfectly nice about it, of course.

"Oh, good, Alma's here," his grandmother said brightly.

Cole nodded absently as his gaze swept over the small crowd gathered in little groups on the lawn of the Augsburg public library. "And so is Emily," he replied as he took in the long length of her jean skirt and how she'd left the top buttons of her Hawaiian shirt undone so that everyone could have a delightful glimpse of her cleavage.

"Remember your promise, Cole," Grams admonished as she waved to another silver-haired lady.

"I will. In fact," he added, "apologizing is the very first thing I'm going to do. If you'll excuse me?"

She beamed up at him. "Of course, dear. And thank you."

He smiled, planted a quick kiss on her cheek and then stepped off the sidewalk and headed across the lawn toward his tall, curvy prey.

Just when she'd become aware of him, he couldn't say, but she watched him advance on her, pursed her lips and then took a long slow sip from her red plastic cup. Her gaze never left his. As he came to a stop in front of her, she arched a perfectly winged brow and sweetly asked, "Are you here to make sure I don't run off with the library's late fees?"

He had to give her credit for being quick-witted. But then again, successful con men—and women—were notorious for being able to think on their feet. He took a breath and cleared his throat. "I'm here to apologize for the way I behaved this morning and to see if perhaps we might be able to start all over again on a better foot."

Her brow inched higher and one corner of her mouth twitched. "Ida laid into you, huh?"

"I'd already come to the conclusion that I'd been an ass." Not exactly the truth, but it was the smart thing to say. "Grams came home soon after that and very quickly reinforced my thinking on the whole thing."

She took another sip of her drink, then studied him, her green eyes dark and serious. "Just for the record, I didn't say a word to Ida about our…exchange."

"She made sure I knew that," he assured her. "Apparently she was only a few steps out of the office when we picked up where we'd left off when she came in. She overheard and stopped in her tracks to eavesdrop."

"Just so that you know that I'm not a lowlife ratter-outer."

As though that was even in the top ten of her sins. "Ida is right," he went on. "I was rude and I really am sorry." He stuck out his hand. "Truce?"

Was it his imagination, or did she lift one brow ever so slightly? Did she suspect his real motives for making nice with her?

"Apology accepted," she said, putting her hand in his and wrapping her fingers around it.

He had a vague thought about how perfect her grip was, but his ability to analyze why melted away as a warm current surged up his arm to his shoulder and then flooded through every fiber of his body.

A buzz, his mind whispered in awe. *An honest to God electric buzz.* How long had it been since…?

"Shall we get something to eat?"

Called back to reality, he blinked and took his cue.

He released her hand and tried to look as though he'd been totally unaffected by the physical contact.

She smiled up at him and there was no uncertainty about the arch of her brow this time. And neither was there any mystery as to what she was thinking. She knew full good and well that she'd sizzled his socks. He could see the amusement sparkling in her eyes.

"I've heard," she said silkily, "that Alma Rogers makes the best fried chicken in the county."

He ran her statement through his mind. Twice. No, he hadn't imagined it; the tone in her voice was unmistakable and the message that eddied through her words was crystal clear. He smiled and wondered if for the rest of his life the words "fried chicken" would translate to "let's get naked."

"Well, let's go judge for ourselves," he said, stepping to the side and motioning for her to lead the way toward the buffet tables set up under the library's giant old elm trees. Falling in beside her, he placed his hand in the small of her back and savored the warmth that radiated through him as he added, "If food hasn't come out of a drive-through window or been delivered by a waiter in the last fifteen years, I haven't had any."

She looked up over her shoulder at him. "I gather you don't get back home much."

Back home? "I've never lived in Augsburg," he clarified. Even to his own ears he sounded critical, so to save himself, he quickly added, "And Grams moved here just a few years ago—five, I think—when the dance company finally forced her to retire."

She handed him a paper plate from the stack at the end of the table and a bundle of napkin-wrapped plastic silverware, forcing him to take his hand off her back. The tingling warmth in him quickly ebbed away. Maybe if he crowded her at the serving table, brushed up against her not-so-accidentally… He took a half step before the voice of reason growled from the back of his brain. He froze in place and took a slow, steadying breath. An inviting smile, a silky voice and one sultry innuendo…. Geez, if there was a con artist Hall of Fame… He was beyond pathetic for letting himself get sucked in so easily, so quickly.

"Really? Listening to Ida talk," she said brightly as she selected a crispy drumstick from the heaping roaster of chicken, "I had the distinct impression that Augsburg was a long cherished ancestral home."

As far as he was concerned, Augsburg was nothing more than a bump in the road he was forced by family duty to visit once—or if things went to hell in a handbasket—twice a year. But actually saying so wouldn't be a good strategic move in his campaign to be a paragon of pleasantness. He followed her, putting a chicken breast on his plate and saying, "Grams's sister, my great-aunt Imogene, married a local man whose family was waiting here for God to invent dirt. Since he wasn't about to move on, Imogene lived here all of her married life. Which was a long time. They didn't have any kids and when she passed away, she left the house to Grams.

"Personally," he went on, "my recommendation was

for Grams to sell it or rent it out as an income-producing property, but she very conveniently went deaf on the whole deal, sold her New York condo instead, and then packed up everything she owned and moved here. She says she likes being able to see from one end of town to the other. As for why, I don't have a clue."

"Oh, I do," his companion claimed, plopping a big scoop of homemade potato salad on her plate. She attacked the platter of sliced tomatoes next as she added, "The older people get, the more they tend to find larger spaces confusing and disorienting. Smalling down their world makes everything more predictable and less stressful for them. I guess I've never really thought of Ida as being old enough for those to be real concerns for her."

"Are you some sort of an expert on old people?" he asked, opting for coleslaw and a pretense of innocent inquiry.

The afternoon sunlight glinted softly in her blond curls as she shook her head and picked up another serving spoon. "Not really," she admitted, chasing a deviled egg around the plate. "What I know about the elderly comes from practical experience. My grandmother moved in with us when I was a teenager. For her, the final straw was the stress of driving in a bigger city. It's just too intense for most older people."

"Well, yeah. It's too intense for *me*. Does that make me an oldster?"

She paused to look over at him—and look him over. "Not hardly."

Okay, so he knew that it was really stupid to be

turned on by her open approval, but the thinking part of his anatomy was a full two ticks behind the rest of him—the rest of him that believed that nothing logical should ever get in the way of having a well-hello-there good time. Yep, by the time his brain had kicked in, it was too late; *his* smile of approval had made the effort pointless.

Grinning, she put down the spoon, reached out to snag the egg with her fingers and then plopped it onto her plate. She flicked the tip of her pink tongue over her fingertips, then laughed softly and asked, "Where do you live?"

"Kansas City," he supplied, quickly deciding to run with the whole thing for now and deal with her possible ulterior motives later. His basic plan, after all, was to keep her close. Real close was even better. "The town of Blue Ridge, to be precise," he went on. "In a two-bedroom, two and a half bath condo with a view of nothing in particular."

"Sounds like a regular real estate dream come true."

Clearly not to her, though. He shrugged and helped himself to the tomatoes. "It's a decent investment property. I'm not there very much so resale value is all I really care about."

"Ida mentioned that you travel a lot. Are you in sales?"

"I'm a venture cap—" The sudden blast of cold air nearly knocked the plate of food out of his hand. He caught it just in time and blinked in amazement at the flurry of paper napkins and plates and plastic lids winging across the library yard. "What the hell?"

"The dry line's here about four hours early," his companion laughingly offered above the wind and flapping storm of debris. Pivoting, she used her hip to keep the plastic wrap from a plate of chocolate chip cookies from being blown away. She set her plate down and while securely covering the cookies, added, "At least it's moving fast. That's kinda good news in the whole big scheme of things."

Women were dashing toward the tables from all over the yard. The men were folding up chairs in their wake. "The *what* line?"

The wind whipping through her blond curls, she turned her head to give him a brief, but puzzled look. "You know, cool dry air slams down on a mass of warm moist air? The wind gust is the leading edge of the storm front. Wicked bad nasty stuff usually rides on the back edge of the dry line."

"But—" He gripped his plate with both hands as another wind gust tried to strip it from his grasp. He looked up through the whipping leaves of the trees overhead. "There isn't a cloud in the sky."

"Look in the direction the blast came from."

He did as she'd instructed. Wicked bad nasty… Yeah, that pretty well described the flashing mass of greenish-black sky barreling at them from the west. He'd add deadly and mean and brutal to the list, too. "I take it that the picnic's over."

"Good looks and keenly observant, too."

He grinned. Good-looking, huh? Now, why her appreciation for his handsome self mattered was beyond him. It wasn't as though he hadn't heard compliments all his life. But still… He watched her lean over the table to put a lid on the potato salad container.

"You might want to finish loading up your plate before they get all the lids on," she said, interrupting his appreciation of her sexy curves. She'd no sooner made the suggestion than a speedy little old lady whisked away the potato salad container. The coleslaw was carted off a half second later by another equally fast and ruthlessly determined elderly woman. The cookie plate was gone in the same fraction of time. A blue-haired lady slammed a lid on the big roaster pan full of chicken and then stepped back to let her husband haul the mass of metal and poultry off the table and toward the cars parked along the street. For an old guy, he covered the ground in really good time.

"Well, okay, that's no longer an option," Emily Raines said, chuckling as she straightened and tried to push her hair out of her eyes.

"Good God, it's like someone yelled, 'Raid'!"

She tipped her head back and laughed outright. The sound was full and throaty, genuine and full of life. He more felt it than he heard it. At least that's the way it seemed. The comfortable, almost settling warmth that had instantly bloomed deep in the center of his chest at her amusement didn't fade as the sound of her laughter trailed off. Marveling, he watched her lift her partially filled dinner plate just enough to pull the tablecloth from underneath.

"You probably need to get Ida home before the rain gets here," she said, giving the cloth a vigorous shake.

Grams! What a lousy grandson he was. He quickly looked around the library yard, half expecting to see that she'd been trampled into the grass by the geriatric stampede. "She's over by the front steps, stacking chairs," he said in relief. He stepped over to a metal barrel trash can and dropped his plate into it, asking, "Do you need help with anything?"

"I'm fine for now, thanks." She tossed down the folded tablecloth and yanked the one off the next table in the line. "But if you want, once you get Ida home, you can come back and help us carry the tables and chairs back into the library storage room."

"Okay. I'll be right back."

"I'll be right here." She laughed again, more softly this time, but the warm fullness in his chest wasn't any less for the difference. "Somewhere."

He nodded, forced himself to tear his gaze away from the windblown opening of her shirt front and turned away. He was a half dozen steps away and still impressed with how sheer a bra could be when she called out, "Hey, Cole!"

He turned around just in time to see her pull her hand from the pocket of her jean skirt.

"You guys walked down from the house. It'll be easier on Ida if you drive her home." Before he could say anything, she tossed him a set of keys. "Green Range Rover on the north side of the library. And don't mess with my radio station!"

Grinning, he saluted her command and then turned away to make his way across the lawn. "Hey, Grams," he called as he reached the library steps. He held up the keys for her to see and jangled them. "How about a chauffeured ride home before the storm breaks?"

She smiled and glanced uptown the six blocks to where his red Porsche was parked in the drive of her house. Her gaze came back to him, a mischievous sparkle in her eyes. "You haven't stolen a car, have you?"

"Emily has loaned us hers so neither one of us has to see if we can do the hundred-yard dash in under fifteen seconds."

"I take it that your apology was accepted?"

"She was very nice about it."

"That's because she's a very nice young lady," his grandmother assured him, waving goodbye to her friends.

Cole fell in beside her, cupping her elbow to steady her as they crossed the lawn and made their way toward the Range Rover. Nice? Yeah, he'd have to allow that Emily had good social skills. The jury was still out on how deep that niceness went, though. It could all be part of the con-artist show. After all, people weren't generally inclined to give their Social Security checks and life savings to strangers who were rude and unpleasant.

Of course, if he had to make a bet one way or the other at this point... Okay, he was usually a good judge of people so, yeah, he'd be willing to put a small amount down—a couple of grand, max—on Emily Raines being a sincerely nice person all the way to the center of her lovely bones.

Time would tell whether or not he should up his ante on her in that regard. Of one thing he was absolutely sure right this moment, though. He'd put about ten grand on her for being the most intriguing woman he'd met in a long, long time. And while he was at it, and as long as he was being honest, he'd put another twenty on keeping her close as eventually turning out to be one of best short-term romantic decisions he'd ever make in his life.

He jangled the keys in his hand and smiled. It was really nice of the weather to have helped him out. There was way more potential in a private dinner for two than a public picnic for fifty and he had every intention of making the most of the unexpected opportunity he'd been handed.

Emily stopped on the top of the library stairs, waiting for Cole to close the door behind them and join her. *Decision, decisions. To take a chance or to play it safe. It's do or die time. For today, anyway.*

He'd be back to shadow her tomorrow. Odds were that he wasn't going to give up his suspicions overnight without some sort of real effort on her part. She'd made a bit of progress in disarming him as they'd made their way down the picnic table. She could press on and hope she didn't come off as pressing too hard, too fast. Or she could just let it go for the night and take another run at him tomorrow.

"Is the door locked?" she asked, watching the wall of shimmering silver coming in from the northwest.

"Yep."

Oh, what the hell. "We have about two minutes before we're drenched," she told him. "Do you want me to run you up to Ida's in the Rover? Or would you like to come over to my place? I can put together a bistro-esque meal. Nothing fancy. Certainly not as good as the meal we had to throw in the trash, but it's something."

"A can of chicken noodle soup with my grandmother or any kind of fare with a gorgeous blonde. Strikes me as a no-brainer."

"Then c'mon," she called, dashing down the steps and toward her car, hoping that everyone in town was glued to their TVs, watching the weather radar, and not the least bit interested in looking out their windows to see her and Cole Preston heading off together to her place. Not that she really cared if they did, she admitted to herself with a smile as she climbed behind the wheel and put the key into the ignition.

Cole dropped into the passenger seat and pulled his door closed as she cranked over the engine. Rap music blasted out of the Rover's speakers.

She punched the power button—hard—and the torture instantly ended. "You messed with my radio station."

He grinned. "I wouldn't have thought of it if you hadn't mentioned it."

Chuckling, she backed the car out of the parking space and headed for her driveway at the other end of the downtown block. It took all of a whole minute to cover the distance. It took just shy of another minute to let them into the warehouse and make their way to the elevator.

The outer doors slid open as soon as she pushed the call button. She was pushing back the scissor gate when a heavy roll of thunder rattled the windowpanes and the man behind her asked incredulously, "How old is this thing?"

"I think Mr. Otis himself installed it," she answered over the hammering arrival of the rain and leading the way in. "But it was inspected and serviced last year. It'll get us to the second floor just fine."

He pulled the scissor gate closed. "It's an unexpected trip to the basement I'm worried about."

"Life is supposed to be an adventure." She pushed the button to take them up. "A bit of danger makes it extra interesting."

"True."

She thought he held his breath until the elevator doors opened again, but couldn't really be sure. There was no doubt about his reaction when she opened the door to her apartment, though.

Three

"As digs go, it's not much, I know," she offered, hanging her car keys on the cup hook someone had long ago screwed into the wall next to the doorjamb. "I've been traveling light for years."

"You have the basics," he observed, his gaze skimming over the sofa, the one end table and the thrift-store coffee table as he walked into the main room. She saw his appraisal move through the open bedroom door to take in the queen-size bed and single nightstand. "All the rest of the stuff people pack into their houses is mostly in the way."

"Thanks, but you don't have to be nice. I know that it looks like there ought to be a Gideon Bible in the nightstand and the Rescue Mission's free meal and mandatory prayer service schedule taped to the back of the front door."

She laughed outright as he automatically looked over his shoulder. "Made you look!" At his chagrined smile, she moved into the kitchen, saying brightly, "Have a seat and I'll put together a quick something to eat. Do you drink wine?"

"Every chance I get."

"Any preferences?" she asked, collecting items from her sparse cupboards. "I have a Zin and a Merlot. We're having fruit and cheese and marginally fancy crackers."

"I'm not a wine snob," he promised as he settled into a corner of the big brown leather sofa, one of her only two brand-new, never-been-used-by-anybody-else furniture purchases. "Whatever you want is fine by me."

Deciding that she'd take both and let him choose, she put the bottles and a corkscrew on a tray with a pair of cheap wineglasses.

"Great windows."

"They're the only redeeming feature to the place." She paused in her collecting to smile at the four huge windows spanning the front wall of the living room. Ten feet high, four feet wide with thick, carved moldings and perfectly sized window seats... Looking at them always gave her hope, always reminded her that the rest of it—the leak-stained ceiling, the long past faded wallpaper on the walls and the plumbing that groaned and moaned like a moose in distress—could be fixed, could be brought up to the standards set by the windows.

Emily shook her head and went back to the task at hand. "When the gust front came through, I'd just asked you what you did for a living," she said, pulling open the refrigerator. "You didn't get a chance to really tell me."

"I'm a venture capitalist."

"Which is what, exactly?" she asked as lightning flashed bright white outside the windows and thunder boomed in the near distance.

"My specialty is providing money for start-up or expanding businesses," he answered above the noise of the storm outside. "I do the research and crunch the numbers and if it's all good, we draft a contract and I write a check. Then I stand back and let them do what they do. After a set period of time, they pay me back with interest."

"And you have to travel a lot to do this?"

"Absolutely. I never invest without meeting the borrowers in person and laying my own eyes on the operation. I have more frequent flyer miles than your average airline pilot."

"Ah," she challenged, slicing a block of cheddar cheese, "but do you know all the flight crews by name?"

"My pilot is Bob. My copilot is Randy and my flight attendant is Collette."

"You have a private plane?"

"A Cessna Citation."

A rich man.... Obscenely rich. He'd probably never in his life been in an apartment this tacky. And she was serving him some slightly too old green grapes, and Monterey Jack and cheddar cheese with crackers out of box decorated with elves. With five-bucks-a-bottle wine to wash it all down. "Your ventures obviously return a good deal of capital," she offered as she carried the tray of poor peasant fare into the living room.

"I do well enough," he replied, watching her set their pathetic excuse for dinner on the coffee table. He slid forward on the sofa and took the merlot and the corkscrew off the tray while adding, "I don't think my father would be at all disappointed in what I've done with my inheritance."

"Has he been gone long?" she asked, taking her conversational cue as she sat down beside him and snagged a piece of the Jack.

"Seven years. He was a heart surgeon who, in a cruel and ironic twist, died of a massive coronary."

"What about your mom?" she asked as she wondered just how many bottles of wine a person had to open before they got as smooth at it as he was.

"My parents divorced when I was in high school. My mother died my sophomore year of college. Ten years ago this spring."

"I'm so sorry," she offered in all sincerity.

He shrugged and poured the wine. Handing her the glass, he said, "I never have been able to understand why a woman who couldn't swim would sign up for a white-water rafting expedition."

"Maybe she was trying to overcome a fear of water."

"Who knows. She didn't talk to me about much of anything except alimony payments and child-support checks." He poured himself a glass of wine, returned the bottle to the tray and leaned back into the sofa. "What about your parents? Still living?"

"Living very well, actually. Mom teaches textile arts at the University of New Mexico at Albuquerque and Dad teaches high school Social Studies."

"Are they cool?"

Emily grinned around the rim of her glass. "Your regular Kum Ba Yah–singing sort of hippie holdovers. It was *so* embarrassing when I was a teenager. Add in my grandmother who, in her last year or so, thought she was living in a clothing-optional world..." She shook her head, remembering, and then lifted her glass in salute to the sweet insanity of her comparatively happy family. "Looking back, it really wasn't as awful as it seemed at the time. I probably should have risked having at least a few slumber parties."

He nodded and leaned forward to make himself a cracker and cheddar sandwich. "Why didn't you follow your parents in the education business?"

"Hey, it wasn't for a lack of trying," she assured him. "My first degree is in secondary education with an emphasis in fine arts. But, just in case you haven't been paying attention to the whole cultural trend thing, funding for art education isn't exactly at the top of the priority list for most school boards these days." She shrugged and took a sip of wine.

"So, throwing good money after bad," she went on as he ate, "I went back for my masters in fine arts. Halfway through I did a summer internship on a restoration project funded jointly by the Smithsonian and the

Rockefeller Foundation. I let them talk me into going in the special projects direction."

"What sort of projects do they do?"

"All kinds, all sizes, all over the country," she supplied, taking a cracker from the plate. "Historic preservation, the performing arts, the visual arts, the sciences in support of the arts. The most famous Rockefeller project is Williamsburg, Virginia, of course. Restoring the historic city, not building the theme park."

"I was wondering."

"Sure you were," she said, chuckling. "I did my internship working on a stained glass window project in the National Cathedral in Washington, D.C., and then on a railroad depot restoration in Seattle. I can't tell you all of the places I've worked since then."

"Your basic nomadic lifestyle."

At least he hadn't said *gypsy.* Nomads ranked considerably higher on the Homeless Integrity Index. "Yeah," she allowed, "I've pretty much lived out of a suitcase for the last few years. Have toolbox, will travel and all that. Which is cool in that I've seen a lot more of America than most people have. If you want a restaurant recommendation along any road, or in any city, just ask me."

He grinned, amusement sparkling in his dark eyes as he met her gaze in good-natured challenge. "Okay. San Francisco."

"Forget the sit-down places. Eat your way along Fisherman's Wharf. Your dollar goes further and you get a whole bunch of great eats. The clam chowder there is awesome. The best I've ever had."

"How are their crab cakes?"

"If you want crab cakes you need to go to Annapolis, Maryland. I don't remember the name of the place, but you can't miss it. Two-story clapboard on the water. It's yellow with brown trim. The best crab cakes in the world. Way more crab than cake. And when you're done eating, you can go over to the Naval Academy and sign up for the tour. They have John Paul Jones in the basement of the chapel."

"Who?"

"John Paul Jones," she repeated. At his cocked brow, she ventured, "The Bonhomme Richard versus the H.M.S. Serapis? There's a famous painting of the battle." He shook his head and she sighed. "American Revolutionary War?"

"I was a finance major with a minor in economics."

"John Paul Jones is the one who said 'I have not yet begun to fight.'"

"Oh, okay," he declared happily, his smile wide. "Why didn't you just say so?"

She rolled her eyes and went on. "Anyway, they have his sarcophagus in a rotunda under the chapel at the Academy. It's a really cool marble deal. Very Davey Jones and Neptune-esque. You do know who Davey Jones is, don't you?"

"Of course." He chuckled and reached for another slice of cheap cheese. "He played with the Monkees. He was the short English guy."

"You're culturally hopeless."

His laugh said he didn't much care. "You know, if

the artist gig doesn't work out, you can be a travel agent. Or a tour guide."

"I guess a person should always keep their options open."

"Are you working on a stained glass project around here?"

He really was good at the pumping for information deal. Very smooth, very easy and conversational. "I have one on the table at the moment. It came in special freight two days ago. But that's it. Nothing local for the time being. I'm a little bit otherwise engaged for the next few weeks. The grand opening is scheduled for the fifteenth of June and there's a ton of work to do between now and then."

He cocked a brow in a silent but eloquent "no kidding" response. "So tell me," he said aloud. "How'd a girl from New Mexico and who's traveled all over the country end up putting down roots in Kansas?"

"I came here last year to repair a church window down in Wichita and took a few day trips on the weekends. One of them was on the Fourth of July. Augsburg has the best, the absolute best, fireworks display you've ever seen. If you can stretch out your visit this time to be here for it, I promise you won't be disappointed."

"I'll give it a shot," he causally offered in the way of commitment. "At the moment, I don't have any crises on the radar, but it's the stuff under the radar that always nails you. So what made you decide to live here between annual fireworks extravaganzas?"

"Real estate here is an incredible bargain and—"

"That's because there's no demand for it," he interrupted with a chuckle. "If it weren't for the weekend tourists, this town would be dead."

"Kansas City will grow this way," she offered confidently. "In twenty years I'll be able to sell my place at an embarrassingly huge profit."

"Twenty years is a long time to wait for a return on an investment."

She shrugged. "Money isn't everything. There's also the logistical considerations. With Kansas being in the middle of the country, it's a shorter flight to anywhere from here. The less time I have to spend in airports and making flight connections, the better. Aside from that..."

She took a quick sip of wine. "Big cities are nice and all. There's lots to see and do. But in the end... Well, I suppose that for me the bottom line is that I can visit big cities anytime I want, but I like living in a place where they call me by name when I walk into the grocery store."

With a quiet snort, he countered, "There are no secrets in a small town."

"True. But that's really not a problem if you're not doing anything that you wouldn't want everyone to know about. Or if you don't give a damn if they do know."

"You have a point. I prefer to remain anonymous while shopping, though."

"Why?"

"It keeps things simple."

Emily chuckled. "I've got to say that I've never considered saying hello to people to be a real complicated social transaction."

"To each his own. I buy a quart of milk, I pay for it, I leave the store, I go home and drink it."

"All alone," she teased in a pitying tone.

"I didn't say that," he drawled. "You're presuming."

She leaned toward him and said in her best imitation of a prosecutorial voice, "If you weren't going home to an empty house, you probably wouldn't be the one buying the milk. And if you were sharing, you'd be buying a gallon, not a quart."

"I'm not a monk."

"I didn't say you were." No one would ever say such a thing. Not once they caught a whiff of that incredible cologne he wore. She'd bet money his was called something like "Yeah, I'm That Good."

He considered her a moment, his eyes sparkling and his smile quirking slowly. "Do you buy milk by the gallon or by the quart?"

She laughed and confessed, "I buy it by the *pint.*"

"Are you a nun?"

"Not unless they've *really* changed the rules," she answered through her laughter. With a sip of wine to sober her, she added, "I've never been a big fan of milk. Positively un-American, I know, and I can't tell you how often I've regretted the fact that I'll never be asked to do one of those mustache ads, but a little bitty splash on cereal once or twice a week is pretty much it for me."

"So there's no significant male other?"

Interesting. Whether or not she had a boyfriend wasn't at all relevant to the Fleecing Granny Investigation he was conducting. Had they crossed a trust line? "Well, my dad's pretty significant to me, but there's no boyfriend," she said. "And there hasn't been in I don't know how long. Is there a significant female other for you?"

He pursed his lips for a long moment and then answered, "I'd describe her as decidedly casual and mostly convenient."

"Geez, you're such a romantic." And way more direct than she'd expected.

"It's never really been necessary."

Yeah, believing that wasn't the least bit of a stretch. "Did they call you Mr. Lucky in high school?"

"Naw. I was…" He shifted his shoulders back and bobbed his head while looking at her through his lashes. He dropped his voice extra low and said, "The Stallion."

She couldn't help herself. She fell back into the sofa, laughing so hard she almost spilled her wine.

"So," he said, his voice sounding tight. He paused, cleared his throat, and tried again. "So why did you decide to give up the road to buy this building and make it into a *fine…arts…center?*"

"Well, it's kind of a long, complicated story."

He reached for the merlot bottle. "As it happens, I don't have a curfew tonight. More?"

She held out her glass and let him pour a generous amount into it before she began, "There's a church up in Wiebeville that—"

"Wee-bee-ville?" he asked, his grin wide and the mouth of the bottle poised motionless above his glass as he looked at her.

"Founded by Mr. Franz Wiebe a hundred-plus

years ago. It's a cute little town about forty miles north of here that's pretty much a retirement community these days. All the old farmers turn the homestead over to the next generation and move into town. They have a church that's listed on the National Historic Register. *Gorgeous* stained glass windows." She shook her head. "Hail the size of golf balls… Not a good thing."

He emptied the last of the wine into his glass and settled his back into the corner of the sofa, angling his long legs partially across the center cushion. "And they called you in to fix them."

"Yep. In the dead of this past January."

"Were you *that* desperate for work?"

"No," she corrected. "That busy. But it wasn't as miserable as you might think. Cold, yes, but definitely not as boring as I thought it was going to be."

"Boring?" he said, brightening. "Why, Miss Raines, I distinctly remember you saying—mere moments ago—that you prefer living in small towns."

"There's a big difference between small and oh-dear-God-just-shoot-me."

"Oh, yeah? What would it be?"

She ignored his sarcasm. "I'll have you know that Wiebeville is one of the most happenin' places on the prairie. They have a kick-butt, state-of-the-art senior center. Every Monday night is polka night. Second and fourth Tuesday is big band or swing. They vote to decide which."

"No square dancing?"

"Friday night. *And* Sunday afternoon. All that dancing is good for the heart and for keeping the bones strong, the muscles toned, you know. I think most of them could outrun me on my best day."

His gaze… There was something different about it as he looked at her. A kind of deepening, settling. Not that it was a dark thing. Not at all. More like an acceptance, a certainty of… Something right? No… Something…

Emily took a quick, healthy drink of wine and deliberately put her mind back on track. "During the daytime hours the seniors have all kinds of art activities. Painting and ceramics. Woodcarving and woodworking and model making. Weaving and quilting and you name it. Everyone comes and goes as they please. Mostly they come in right after breakfast, stay through lunch—there's an ethnic cuisine cooking class three days a week and leftovers on the other two—and they take off for home about four to eat supper and to get into the dance outfit *du noir*."

He gave her a lopsided smile. "Any clothing-optional devotees in the bunch?"

"No, and that's exactly what I noticed," she supplied excitedly. "Everyone is mentally alert and interested in life. Oh, yeah, one of their favorite conversations is about the latest meds their doctor has them on and what tests they're scheduled for, but the important part is that they're having that conversation while they're turning a wooden bowl on the lathe, putting a quilt on a frame and buckling up their square-dance shoes. They're active. They're involved. The creative parts of their brains are kept engaged. They're alert and mentally sharp and young at heart."

"And so you decided that Augsburg needed a place like that, too."

It would be easy and safe to take the story leap he offered, to blow right on past the hard to believe part. Easy, yes, but only in the short run.

"Actually, I wrote a letter to the area newspaper, complimenting the taxpayers for funding such a great place for the retirees. And then I waxed a bit poetic about how wonderful the world would be if there were more senior centers in rural areas to keep our aging parents and grandparents involved in life and physically and mentally active for as long as possible.

"The next week a man walked into the church while I working and asked me if I was Emily Raines. I said I was and he handed me an envelope, and then walked out. Inside the envelope was a clipping of my letter to the editor and a cashier's check for fifty thousand dollars."

He lowered his chin and tipped his head slightly to the side. "Who was the guy?'

"I have absolutely no idea. None," she admitted. "No return address on the envelope. Nothing at all to give me even a little bitty hint as to who my Secret Santa might be."

"Someone just gave you fifty thousand dollars out of the blue."

"Yeah. I know. I didn't believe it, either. I looked at that cashier's check at least a dozen times a day for a week, just trying to wrap my brain around it."

She shrugged and sighed. "And I eventually decided that since it came with a clipping of my Wouldn't It Be Lovely letter, I was supposed to use the money to set up a senior citizen fine arts center somewhere."

"You could have given the money to a foundation and specified that the interest be used for the support of existing senior programs."

"If Secret Santa had wanted to do that with the money, he would have done it himself," she countered with a shake of her head. The room moved back and forth a little longer than her head did. "I honestly think he gave it to me because he wanted to invest in my vision of spreading Wiebeville across America."

"Why'd you pick Augsburg?"

"Lots of elderly. Well, and the man who owned this building was only asking thirty grand for it."

"You got took."

"I did not," she asserted with a chuckle. "Between the two floors, I have almost twenty thousand square feet and, except for this apartment, all of it is wide-open space for doing whatever I want with it. Don't forget the elevator, either. And I talked him down to twenty-two five and into paying half of the closing costs."

He lifted his gaze to the stained ceiling tiles. "What kind of shape is the roof in?"

"That's an old stain," she explained. "The roof in this section is about fifteen years old and it's holding up fairly well. The rest of it.... Okay, it leaks like a sieve." She turned on the sofa to look out the front windows.

The rain rolled past in gray sheets, so thick and fast that she couldn't see the park across the street.

She turned back to face him, realizing as she did that she'd had a tad too much wine, too fast. She looked at her glass, noting that only a sip or two remained. "If it rains like this for very much longer, I'll be able to have a swimming party in the front office. B.Y.O.F."

"B.Y.O.F.?"

"Bring your own floaties." She grinned, finished the contents of her glass and then leaned forward to put it on the coffee table. Picking up some crackers and a few slices of cheese, she added, "I have some roofing bids and I'll get it taken care of in the next week or so."

"Ten thousand square feet of roofing… You don't have enough of the Secret Santa money left to pay for a new roof."

"I have a piggy bank," she assured him.

"Unless your piggy bank is the size of a Hummer, you're severely undercapitalized."

"I'll be just fine." Well, financially, anyway, she allowed as she very carefully folded a slice of cheese in half. Functionally… Hopefully the wine was done creeping up on her. It would be really embarrassing to fall off the sofa. She needed to eat something. And focus. She needed to keep her mental focus until the fuzziness wore off. What were they talking about? Hummers the size of pigs. No, that was backwards. Piggy banks. Costs.

"I plan to start small and add stuff over time as I can afford it," she said, feeling incredibly pleased with picking up where she figured she'd left off. "It doesn't take much to have a polka night, you know. An MP3 player loaded with Big Joe Polka tunes and a decent pair of speakers, some munchies and a cooler full of well-iced brewskies… Hey, we're good to dance 'til dawn. Or until the cops come to break up the party. Whichever comes first."

"You could ask for donations."

"For what? The beer?" Was it the wine, or was his smile considerably more quirked than before?

"The roof, Emily. You could ask for donations for the roof."

"No. It's really bad form to ask people to chip in to buy their own gift."

He chuckled and smoothly eased out the corner of the sofa to set his glass of wine on the table beside hers. "How about applying for foundation grants? I hear that they love this sort of thing."

She ate a cracker and two pieces of cheese while she nodded like a bobblehead dog on the rear window deck of a '62 Chevy Impala. It was hard to swallow it all down, but she immediately felt better for having made the effort.

"Foundations run on strict timetables for applications," she explained, folding another piece of the cheese. "There's a…well, a *season* and you have to have your paperwork ready to go in the second it opens. Miss it and you have to wait until next year. I didn't get the Secret Santa money in time to be part of this year's charitable dash for the cash.

"My friend Beth—she's an accountant—is working on some applications for next year. I'm going for the woodworking machines. You know, table saws and planers and lathes. That sort of stuff. I'm also going for a professional kitchen. The rest of what's needed is small-ticket stuff that I can buy on sale at a hobby store up in Kansas City."

"What about insurance, taxes, utilities?" he asked as he pulled a clump of grapes off the main stem. "How are you going to pay those expenses?"

"This year it's coming out of the piggy bank. Next year…I'll figure it out. Maybe I can go for some operating money through a grant."

"Is your piggy bank a real piggy bank?" he asked, handing her the grapes. "Or is that what you call your investment portfolio?"

"It's a savings account at a reputable bank." Given the look on his face at that announcement… It was nice to know that she might not be the only one falling off the sofa. She ate a grape and waited for him to collect himself.

"Earning what? Two percent a year?"

"I actually have no idea. I think I made about twenty dollars in interest last year. Enough, anyway, that the IRS wanted to know about it. *And,*" she added confidently, "it's FDIC insured."

"Theoretically," he declared. "It's also not working for you as hard as it could be."

"Well, if you're suggesting that I add 'learn how to play the stock market without losing my shirt' to my list of things to do this week… Sorry. I'm already signed up for the 'how to sand and refinish wood floors' class."

"I've seen you with a floor sander. You need the class...bad."

"And basic bathroom plumbing and simple tiling come right after that," she told him, popping another grape in her mouth. "Restrooms are a very high priority for the elderly."

"You need to let a professional invest your money for you."

"I agree. But right now I need the cash on hand. I can't afford to have it tied up for the long haul."

"There's this thing called day trading...?"

She snorted. And managed to suck a piece of grape skin hard against the back of her throat. Even as her brain was saying what an incredibly uncool thing she'd just done, her cough reflex kicked in. "Unless you're volunteering to do it," she struggled to say through the fit, "you can forget it. I'm totally clueless."

Handing her his wineglass with one hand, he slid close and gently patted her upper back with the other. A sip didn't accomplish anything toward dislodging the peeling, but a second, heftier one, did. "Thanks," she whispered hoarsely, feeling like a complete and utter idiot.

He didn't move away, didn't take his hand from her back when he reached down to his hip and pulled his cell phone out of the holster. Holding it in his free hand, he flipped it open, hit a single button with his thumb and then held it to his ear.

"Hey, Jase," he said a second later. "What you got going on this evening?" There was a short pause during which Emily resisted the urge to lean into him and lay her head on his shoulder.

"Good," he said. "I need the mini station down here."

She breathed deep and decided that his cologne should be made illegal. Or at least available only by prescription.

"Sounds perfect to me. Eight it is. And thanks, Jase." He flipped the phone closed and holstered it, saying, "There, Miss Raines. You may consider yourself as having hired an investment guru."

"Can I afford you?" she asked, tilting her head to look up at his face.

"I don't think the charges will be all that outrageous."

Oh, God. That soft, low rumble of his that melted her bones. She drew a slow breath and kept herself from leaning deeper into the curve of his arm. "Give me a ballpark idea of what kind of fees we're talking about."

He tipped his head and lowered his lips toward hers. She closed her eyes and stopped breathing altogether as his lips slowly, softly and thoroughly took possession of hers. Swaying, she slipped an arm around his neck and held on, savoring the delicious warmth flooding through her.

He drew back just enough to meet her gaze. His smile knowing, his eyes sparkling with amused certainty, he asked, "Steeper than you expected?"

Actually, it wasn't nearly as steep as she was suddenly wanting. No, *needing*. "I can't remember ever enjoying paying a bill quite so much," she replied, threading her fingers through the hair at his nape and hoping it was enough of a blatant-but-just-shy-of-tawdry hint to keep things moving forward. Preferably quickly. Before she exploded—all by herself—right there on the sofa.

His smile quirked slowly. “Oh, yeah?” he whispered as he took his wineglass from her hand and blindly set it on the table. “Wanna make some advance payments on your account?”

“I’d love to,” she admitted, twining her other arm around his neck. He chuckled, put his arms around her waist and drew her against the hard heat of his body. She went, her lips parting beneath his, her senses flooding with a deliciously desperate kind of hunger. She felt him pull her shirttail from her skirt and whimpered in delight as his hands skimmed upwards over her bare skin to undo the hooks on her bra. She was on fire, completely, gloriously, thoroughly—

The 1812 Overture?

At least she wasn’t the only one surprised. Cole abruptly broke their kiss and freed a hand from her shirt, saying, “Sorry,” as he yanked his cell phone from the holster and flipped it open. “Hi, Grams,” he said without preamble. “What’s up?”

His wince at whatever Ida was telling him didn’t take a rocket scientist to interpret.

“Yes, he is. And, yes, it was very nice of him to let you know.”

Augsburg, we have a problem.

“No, of course not. Nothing we can’t pick up again some other time. I’m on my way right now.”

He flipped the phone closed with a heavy sigh. She spared him from having to actually announce that the good times weren't going to roll for them that night. Taking her arms from around his neck, she put some distance between them, saying, "You've been called home to get ready for Jase's arrival."

He sighed hard again, put his hands on his knees and leveraged himself to his feet. "She can't let Jason see the house in such a mess. And she has to bake a cake and freshen the bathroom towels and get the second guest room ready and, and, and." He scraped his fingers through his dark, already tousled hair. "And since he's my employee, I need to go help her be an impressive domestic goddess."

Emily stood, too. Reaching up one arm of her shirt, she grasped the strap of her unhooked bra and pulled it down her arm while she admitted, "I'd pay money to see you in an apron, you know."

"I don't think so," he replied, watching intently as she dragged the other strap down and out. "What else besides an apron?"

"Absolutely nothing at all."

He blinked and grinned at her, arching a brow. "*That* I'd be willing to do."

She laughed, pulled the bra from under her shirt, and dropped the sheer scrap of fabric on the coffee table between them.

His smile disappeared in an instant even as his brow inched higher. Considering the bra, he asked, "How long does it take to bake a cake and freshen towels?"

"Longer than you're hoping," she laughingly replied as she moved around the coffee table and toward the apartment's front door. "But I'll give you a rain check for tonight. Redeemable anytime." She heard him mutter under his breath, but he followed.

"Here," she said, opening the door and handing him her car keys. "Take the Rover to Ida's. You'll drown if you walk. You can bring it back in the morning."

"Thanks." He frowned at the keys and looked up at her, his smile inching back for a moment as though he might be thinking about kissing her good-night.

"I'll see you tomorrow," she said, putting the kibosh on letting him get her wound up for nothing all over again.

He grinned and winked, then nodded and walked off toward the elevator, calling over his shoulder, "I'm really looking forward to it."

She closed the apartment door behind him and leaned her head against the cool wood of the carved doorjamb. Tomorrow. She could wait until tomorrow, she assured herself. She had to wait. She didn't have any other real choice because having Ida catching her climbing through her grandson's bedroom window in the middle of the night would be just too much for a genteel little old lady's heart to take.

Four

Emily considered the pale gray light coming weakly through the warehouse windows and rolled her already cramping shoulders. A night of restless sleep, a good hour of literally sweeping the water out the warehouse front door, of answering a thousand questions about a million details from five electricians all at once... The stuff the dreams of social do-gooders were *not* made of.

She looked at her watch and sighed. Seven minutes. All of seven minutes since the last time she'd checked the time and wondered when Cole was going to get there.

"Pa-thet-ic," she muttered, taking her watch off her wrist and setting it in the open lid of her toolbox. "He'll get here when he gets here," she admonished. "And not one second sooner. So buck it up and get something done while you wait. Nothing sadder than being caught sitting by the phone and waiting for it to ring."

She studied the old, battered stained glass window lying on the table in front of her, her gaze tracing over the lines of solder. Picking out the subtle signs that told her in what order the small glass pieces had originally been put together, she followed the course backward to where the next piece needed to be removed, and then picked up her tools again.

Carefully laying the hot tip of the iron on the solder, Emily slowly melted the joint where three pieces of glass met and then used the scraper she held in the left hand to pull the excess liquid metal off the ancient copper tape below. The silvery stuff pooled on the glass, the molten surface instantly skimming over as it cooled, darkened and eased back to a solid state. She moved the iron to the next juncture and repeated the process, melting, dragging and letting it cool, working steadily to release the individual antique glass shapes from the intricate floral and vine pattern some unknown artist had just as painstakingly assembled over a century ago.

It took several minutes—no more than usual—to completely melt the metal holding the two-inch curved piece of swirled green glass in place. Propping the iron in its insulated holder, she picked up a bare utility blade and inserted it in the sliver of space she'd created and gently leveraged the glass shape free of the pattern. Stepping to the other side of the table, she scraped the old copper foil off all the edges with the blade and then held the piece up to the light.

No cracks, no chips that she could see. "Four down," she said to herself as she wrote the number on the glass piece with a black grease pencil. "Seventy, eighty, ninety or more to go," she added as she laid it on the number four spot of the vellum template she'd made last night. She adjusted how pieces one, two and three laid in relation to four, making sure that all the spaces were equal.

"Sorry to have to bother you, Miss Raines."

She looked up from her work, smiled at the electrician—Mike?—and assured him, "It's not a bother at all. What can I help you with?"

"On that wiring for the woodwork shop you're going to put in... Do you want two outlet receptacles? Or four?"

"What would be your recommendation?" God, was she smooth? Total ignorance and not a sign of it.

"I'd go with four."

"Then four it is."

"Okay," he said, writing on his little notepad. "Let me check to make sure there isn't something else so I don't have to bother you again."

While he flipped through his notes, she moved back around the table to the larger piece.

"I thought you were supposed to be taking a floor sanding class today."

She looked up, grinning, to watch Cole Preston close the distance between them. "Good morning," she said, wondering if he'd ever thought about modeling for a living. Not every man could make a pair of khaki trousers and a light blue oxford shirt look like a million bucks.

"Morning," he replied, stopping a perfectly respectable distance away and dropping her car keys beside the toolbox.

"I don't see anything else, Miss Raines. Thanks."

"Don't hesitate to ask if something else comes up," she called after the departing electrician.

Turning back to Cole, she said, "After I drained the pool in the front office this morning, I gave the sander a shot, but it was an absolute no-go. Everything is way too damp. The dust is miserable, but gum paste is even worse. This weather system is supposed to clear out tomorrow afternoon. Until things dry out, though, there's no sanding, no painting, no staining and certainly no divinity making."

"Divinity?"

"A candy made with egg whites," she explained, propping her hip against the worktable. "Egg whites don't beat up right when there's high humidity. There's no hope for a seven-minute frosting, either. Although I gotta tell you, even under the best weather conditions, I have never been able to make a seven-minute frosting in under fifteen minutes."

He knitted his brows as he fought to keep a smile contained. "Do you suppose I've ever had seven-minute frosting?"

"It's usually on angel food cakes. Frothy and light with soft little peaks. Basically it's the cake version of the meringue on a pie."

"Well, you learn something new every day." His attention went to one of the electricians backing through the warehouse, uncoiling a big spool of yellow wire. "I see that the sparkies aren't worried about working in the damp."

"They're running the new electrical wiring today. They've *sworn* to me that nothing they're doing is hooked up to the juice."

His attention came to back to her. "So what are you working on?" he asked, stepping up to the table beside her and looking down at the battered window.

"It's from a couple in Minneapolis," she explained, breathing deep the delicious scent of him. "They're restoring an old Victorian mansion and the Smithsonian sent them my way. Since I couldn't get there to do the repairs on-site, they crated it up and shipped it to me. Money is no object for these people."

"Apparently. It looks complicated."

"It's not a Stained Glass 101 project, that's for sure."

"It also looks like it's taken a lot of abuse over the years."

"Apparently the mansion has been vacant for the last thirty years or so. Vandals had done a number on it and then some kind, well-intentioned soul thought it would be a good idea to take it out of the window and store it in a damp basement. Why people feel compelled to break glass…"

She shook her head and then resolutely brightened. "By the time I'm done with it, I'll probably have around fifty or so hours and a good grand of new materials in it. Antique glass and reproduction glass are high dollar.

But when it goes home, it'll look every bit as good as the day it was first made."

"Shipping will cost more than the repairs."

"I told you, money is no object here. And speaking of money," she hurriedly added, "I forgot to ask you last night how you want the check made out for the trading you're going to do for me."

"Don't worry about it right now. I set up a separate account under my name and spotted you ten to get started last night. I'll take the seed money out of the proceeds when I transfer the profits to you."

"Ten? I can chip in more than ten bucks. I'm not a total pauper." She grinned and added, "I just look like one."

"Ten *grand*."

There was beholden and then there was *beholden*. "That's a lot of money to loan someone," she protested. "And while I really appreciate it, I have twenty grand in the Secret Santa account that—"

He held up his hand, palm toward her. "You never gamble with what you can't afford to lose," he kindly but firmly advised her. "If your twenty goes up in smoke, you can't get a new roof put on this beast. I've covered you. I can easily afford it. It's a done deal."

In other words, there was nothing left for her to do but be gracious about it. "Thank you."

He smiled. "You're welcome."

Since it was a done deal... "So what stocks do I own?"

"I put you in short on financials before the market opened this morning," he answered crisply and with what sounded like great satisfaction. "I'm trading you long on oil and wheat futures for the time being, but I've set the auto trade program with triggers to sell and go short at the first sign that the bubble is going to pop."

Emily didn't even bother to run any of it over in her mind. She knew it wouldn't make the least bit of difference. She leaned toward him and whispered, "I've never heard Greek before. It's kinda sexy."

So was the incredible warmth radiating from his body. It crossed her mind to simply throw herself against him and be done with any pretense of decorum. She eased away, her sense of deprivation not all that assuaged by the thought that her mother would be pleased that she was behaving like a lady.

He laughed and then said through a wide grin, "We're betting that the banks lose big money and—"

"That's not very nice."

"Nice isn't an investment strategy," he replied, chuckling. "Anticipating whether stocks will go up or down is."

She frowned. "How do you make any money if the stocks you own go down?"

"Okay," he said on a sigh. "Technically, you don't own any shares in the banks. You've borrowed them from someone who does own them with—"

"How do I know this person?"

"They advertise."

"Okay. Go on."

He smiled, closed his eyes for a second and mouthed *thank you.* "All right," he said, returning to his explanation. "You borrow them with the promise that you're going to give them back in a few weeks with a little interest payment. While you have them, you sell them to someone else."

"You can't sell something you don't own." What had he gotten her into? "That's illegal."

"Only outside the stock market."

He sounded so sure of it. Still… "You're kidding me, right?"

"No, I'm not," he said with absolute confidence. "Now, say you've sold the shares for ten bucks each and the price drops to five. You buy them back at five and return the stocks to the guy you borrowed them from. Net profit on the trade itself is five bucks a share. If you traded a thousand shares, what's your profit?"

"A math story problem!" she gasped. Leaning back, she held up her hands between them, her index fingers crossed one over the other. "Get back, Spawn of Satan!"

"It's five grand," he declared, shaking his head and rolling his eyes. "It's also really simple math."

"It sounds too easy. The trading part," she quickly clarified. "Not the math. No math is easy."

"Yes, it is easy to make the money on the trade. Unless you bet wrong on the market direction and the price you buy back at is higher than when you sold. Then you lose not only your shirt, but your pants, socks and underwear, too."

"Ooooh. Strip stock trading," she said, her mind filled with delightful images of Cole Preston at the end of a bad trading day. "You could sell tickets, you know. The Chippendales of Wall Street. Do a little peep-and-tease dance with briefcases."

His eyes sparkling, and fighting back a smile, he cleared his throat and said, "Anyway, we're also betting that the price per barrel of oil keeps going up and that a bushel of wheat does, too. Not, mind you, that I think those are long-term positions. Current price trends in commodities are more a reflection of money looking for a safe haven from the market's volatility. That says speculative bubble to me."

Whatever. She hadn't heard much more than a half of what he'd said. "Ooooh, more Greek," she said on a whimpering sigh. She undid another button on her blouse and fanned her shirtfront. "I'm feeling a little breathless."

"So am I," he admitted, his gaze slowly coming up from her chest. Had he noticed that she wasn't wearing a bra at all this morning? "What time does this crew plan to clear out of here for lunch?"

"They're working through lunch and breaks today because they need to get this done so they can start another job tomorrow."

"Where's a strong union when you need one?" he muttered, scowling down at the stained glass window. He suddenly lifted his head and met her gaze, his eyes smoldering with undisguised desire. "Wanna come over to Grams's place and see my trading desk?"

"Is that anything like asking a girl if she'd like to see your etchings?" she teased, fanning her shirt again.

"In this case, it's a straight translation."

Oh, he was wound tight; she could hear it in his voice, could see the smoldering in his eyes and the tense lines at the corners of his mouth. "I take it that Ida's over at the Senior Center this morning?"

"And planning to play bridge all day."

"I'd *love* to see your trading desk," she admitted, relenting. "Let me get things unplugged and put away. It won't take me any more than a couple of minutes."

Even as she spoke, she bent over to unplug the iron from the outlet. The sensation of his hands boldly skimming up the backs of her jean-clad thighs took her breath away. The heat of his palms as he laid them flat over the curve of her rear and ever so slightly squeezed… Her insides instantly molten and pounding, she straightened and looked at him over her shoulder. "Do that again," she said, her voice husky, "and you're going to get your bones jumped right here in front of God and any sparky that wanders through."

"Life should be an adventure, remember?" he reminded her as she stepped out of his easy reach. "A little danger…"

"Danger is fine," she retorted, retrieving her watch and closing the lid of the toolbox. "Exhibitionism is another thing entirely."

"Then stop bending over like that and tempting me. I'm only human."

And so was she. A human female with apparently no fuse at all. "Let me get my purse out of the apartment and we can go."

He caught her hand and pulled her back, saying, "You're not going to need it."

Did that mean he intended to drive them to Ida's? she wondered as she let him lead her to the elevator. Or did it mean he had his own condoms and that she could keep the ones she'd been carrying around in her purse for the last eon or two? Now that she thought about it, there were probably expiration dates on condoms. Any he had were a sure bet to be at least current. Hers, just as certainly, weren't.

Emily waited until he pulled the scissor doors closed and then punched the down button. The outer doors were barely closed when he suddenly straightened beside her, happily declared, "Hey, I have an idea!" and reached out toward the control panel.

"No!" she cried, catching his arm, knowing exactly what he had in mind and why. "An alarm will go off. And it's *loud*."

He let his arm fall back to his side, muttering regretfully, "Damn. It was a fabulous fantasy."

"No kidding," she agreed on a long, hard sigh. "Short-lived, but reeeallly good."

He looked over at her. The brightness of his smile said it all; he was clearly surprised by her honest reaction and just as obviously intrigued with the possibilities in her being a good sport. "Is there any way we can shut off the alarm?"

"Well, yeah, but not right this moment and not from in here."

"I'll take care of it when we come back," he promised as they reached the first floor and the doors opened.

"Just as a point of information," she offered while he

pushed back the scissor door. "I was wearing a halter top, a short skirt and pair of stilettos in my version."

"Oh, yeah? How short?"

"If I had bent over," she said casually, walking past him out of the elevator, "you would have seen that I wasn't wearing any panties."

He stopped in his tracks. She paused and waited for him to recover his wits. He had to swallow twice before he could get his feet to move. As he reached her side and together they made their way toward the front door, he asked, "How late do you think this electrical crew is going to be here finishing up today?"

Well, there was no grass growing under the feet of the Cole Preston side of her fantasy. "They said probably seven or so," she supplied as they stepped out onto the sidewalk. "Hold on a second."

She called out to the electrician taking a box out of the back of their work van. "John?"

"Yes, ma'am?"

"I'm wondering if I could get you to disconnect the alarm on the elevator while you all are working? When I'm moving stuff between floors and having to prop the doors open for a while, the ringing drives me nuts."

"I'll take care of it for you right now, Miz Raines."

"Thanks, John! I'll be back in a little bit. If there's a problem, I have the cell on."

"That was smooth," Cole said softly as he held open the passenger door of his car for you.

"Hey, the fantasy doesn't include us down in the

basement with me holding a flashlight while you figure out which fuse to pull."

He laughed, closed the door and trotted around to his side of the car. He backed them out of the parking slot and had them pointing toward his grandmother's house when he asked, "What was I wearing in your version of the fantasy?"

"A huge smile."

"That's a given. Other than that."

"Let me see." She wiggled into the curved back of the luxurious leather car seat and closed her eyes. "A gray suit. White shirt. Red tie." She smiled. "Interesting." Opening her eyes, she turned to look at him. "You weren't wearing any underwear, either."

"Well, I do believe in being prepared to seize any opportunity that presents itself."

"I seized first. Boldly, confidently. Just so you know."

Grinning, he said, "That's okay with me," and eased the car into his grandmother's driveway. "It's your elevator. I'm only along for the ride."

"Yeah, well, I have a news flash for you."

He laughed and got out of the car. Knowing that she was perfectly capable of doing the same without gallant male assistance, Emily didn't wait for him to come around and open the door for her. She met him at the headlights and followed him up the steps and into Ida's house.

She wasn't even all the way across the threshold when she saw that her elderly friend's living room had been utterly transformed. The serving buffet that usually sat against the far wall of the living room was gone. So, apparently, were the silver candelabra and the collection of porcelain figurines that normally sat atop it. In the buffet's place was a huge but sleek, minimalist high-tech-looking desk and chair. And on top of the desk's glass top.... Emily counted. Seven flashing monitors, four hard drives and two laser printers. She looked again. No, no partridge in a pear tree.

"Jeez Louise, Cole. Was NORAD having a garage sale? Or is that stuff just on loan?"

"This is my traveling setup," he explained. "Nothing more than the bare minimum."

"So I guess I'm not going to get to watch you call in an air strike, huh? Bummer. Talk about sexy. Even better than Greek."

He chuckled, caught her hand in his and headed across the living room toward Computer Central. "Would you like to see where your account balance is at this point in the day?"

As if she could say no while she was being towed across a beige berber sea? But there was seductive potential in gadgets and blinking lights; she could work with it. "I should probably have a fair idea of just how much I owe you in management fees already."

When he came to a stop in front of the desk, Emily slipped up against his side and wrapped an arm around his waist. He draped an arm over her shoulder and looked down at her, his brow cocked. "You believe in seizing opportunities," she said silkily. "I believe in paying my obligations in full when they're due."

He bent his head. Her heart racing, Emily closed her eyes and parted her lips. The computer dinged. She staggered, he let go of her so fast.

"Have a seat," he commanded, working a mouse across the desktop, his gaze riveted on one of the monitors.

"Since you're the one at the controls," she offered, pulling her blouse back to rights, "shouldn't you be the one sitting in the chair?"

He looked up over his shoulder at her to give her a sheepish grin. "Sitting right now would be more than a little uncomfortable for me."

"Really." She dropped into the chair, wondering if she was the cause, or if he actually got that big of a charge out of trading.

"Yes, really."

Well, she decided, there was only way to find out. She reached out and slowly drew her hand up the hard ridge lying beneath the fly of his khakis. "Do you have a day-trader fantasy?" she asked.

"Apparently you do," he answered, his hand over the now-still mouse, his gaze smoldering and locked with hers. "I'm liking it so far."

"Yes, I can see that." She ran her hand over him again, harder this time. "May I see more?"

He abandoned the mouse, straightened and turned to face her. "Your wish is my command," he said, unzipping.

"Such an accommodating gentleman."

"The jury's out on the gentleman part." He freed himself, then added, "Accommodating… Yes, definitely," as he set about undoing his belt.

She didn't wait for him to get as comfortable as he had in mind. She took him in her hand, stroking down the hardened length and then slowly stroking back up.

"I'll add appreciative, too," he said hoarsely, his hands still as he broadened his stance. She quickened the pace of her strokes and he drew a breath through his teeth. Tipping his head back, he groaned at the ceiling. "That feels so good."

Yes, it did. God, she was climbing the arc herself, her own tension coiling tighter, hotter, and building with the power of his arousal, with every sound he made in the throes of the pleasure she was giving him.

The sound was muffled, but distinct. Emily froze, listening. It was followed by another and then two more in quick succession.

"What?" Cole demanded. "Don't stop!"

The moment of possibility and promise shattered, she drew back quickly and looked up at him. "I hear car doors." The look of disbelief and frustration on his face…

Emily fought the urge to laugh as he growled and made a rather penguin-esque—no, pissed off penguin-esque—trip over to look out the front window.

"Hell!" he cried, whirling back and frantically trying to get himself tucked back behind his trouser fly. "It's Grams and the bridge club!"

Emily leaned back in the chair and stretched out her legs as she watched him arrange himself, tug at his clothes, then put a hand on the back of one of Ida's wingback chairs and stare off in the general vicinity of the crown moldings. Emily sighed softly around a smile. If only he'd had a keg and a parrot....

Outside the window, Ida and three blue-haired ladies were making their way along the front walk. Emily looked back at Cole. "That's your *best* casual I-wasn't-doing-anything pose? Gotta tell ya, it's *not* working for you."

"God," he groaned, his shoulders sagging. He glanced around the room and then moved toward her saying, "Out of the chair."

She did as he commanded, saying, "I thought sitting was uncomfortable for you."

"Not a problem now," he declared crisply as he dropped into the seat and grabbed the mouse. "Grams and her friends coming up the walk took care of it."

Standing behind him, she put her hands on the back of the chair . She leaned close and said softly, "I always wondered what they meant by 'deflationary pressure.' Now I know. You learn something new every day."

"Your economic education was appalling."

Listening to Ida insert her key into the door lock, Emily kissed the curve of his ear and whispered, "Wanna tutor me?"

"You're not helping me here."

"I know," she laughingly admitted as she straightened and focused over his head at the monitor screen right in front of them.

"Cole!" Ida exclaimed happily as she entered the living room. "Emily! What a pleasant surprise, my dears. Are you playing one of those computer games?"

Emily turned to smile at her friend. "Hi, Ida. No

games. Cole's trying to teach me the basics about investing in the stock market. So far I'm proving to be a less than stellar student."

"She's very easily distracted," Cole supplied without looking away from the chart on the computer screen.

"Would we be a distraction to you if we play bridge in the dining room?" Ida asked as her friends trooped past her into the adjacent room. "They fumigated the kitchen at the Senior Center last night and the smell is still just horrendous today. We were hoping we could ignore it, but it's given Gladys a headache."

"No distraction for me at all, Ida," Emily assured her. "I really think that your poor grandson has had his frustration quota met for today and I need to head back to the warehouse to check on the electricians."

"I'll drive you there," he offered, putting his hands on the chair arms and starting to gain his feet.

Putting her hands on his shoulders to stop him, Emily brightly replied, "Thank you for offering, Cole, but the walk will do me good." Before he could protest, she turned and walked away, adding, "Got to keep the muscles toned and the stamina up. You never know when you're going to have to do a marathon."

She stopped at the front door and with a hand on the doorjamb, turned back to find him watching her departure, looking like a man watching the rescue boat sink twenty feet from shore. "Oh, what time did you say for dinner tonight, Cole?"

He instantly brightened and grinned. "I seem to recall that we decided on sevenish."

"Perfect. I'll meet you at Vito's. I'll be the one in the green dress."

"I'm thinking a gray suit, red tie. Would that be too upscale?"

"Sounds perfectly yummy to me." She smiled at his grandmother. "Win big, Ida. Kick their butts."

Ida laughed and Emily left the house, bounding down the stairs and feeling utterly, thoroughly delighted with life. She could only hope that Cole would spend the afternoon trading stocks and making her a huge, huge pile of money for which she would owe him huge, mind-blowing fees.

Making her way down the sidewalk toward her warehouse, she made a mental list of what had to be done in the next few hours. At the very top of it was to make sure that she could still get into her green dress. If she couldn't, she was going to have to make a dash up to Kansas City and find a new one.

Everything else on the list behind the dress was optional. Yeah, clean sheets on the bed, some votive candles and a couple of bottles of chilled white wine would be nice. But they would be damn small consolation at the end of even a slightly disappointing elevator ride.

No, anything less than total fantasy fulfillment was not acceptable. When she walked into Vito's that evening, Cole Preston's jaw was going to hit the linen-covered tabletop. And by the time they finished licking the cannoli cream off each other's fingers, the only challenge would be to hold back until they actually got into the elevator. But once those doors closed…

Yes, life was good and it was only going to get better as the day turned into night. And as the night turned into a dawn they could wake up to wildly, breathlessly celebrate together. Maybe, if the sun were shining like the weatherman had promised it would, they could celebrate its return twice, once wherever they happened to have collapsed in exhaustion in the night, and then…

"Gotta clean the shower," she said as she walked into the warehouse. She stopped, her mind clicking through a household and bedroom inventory list that sent her heart racing in a barely contained panic. She checked her watch and did the calculations. Two hours to Kansas City and two hours back, an hour to get the apartment ready and an hour to get herself irresistibly gorgeous. Yeah, she'd have to make every minute count, but she could do it.

Cole Preston was most definitely worth the effort. Okay, she admitted to herself as the took the elevator up to get her purse and car keys, maybe it wasn't so much Cole Preston himself as it was the promise of a night of hot, torrid, panting, sheet-twisting, world-shattering sex. Cole Preston, Greek god, hunky and every bit as hungry as she was, might well be no more than the icing on the cake.

Not that she was going to spend a lot of time trying to figure it out for sure, she decided as she let herself into her apartment. He was here, he was willing, and there didn't appear to be anything wrong with his ready and able.

She woke up her computer and executed a search.

While the map and directions were printing, she took her sexy green dress out of the closet and gave it a quick try on.

Emily checked her watch. What a difference ten minutes could make. She dropped down on the sofa and tossed the computer printout onto the coffee table, sensing that the impromptu trip was slipping out of her grasp by the second.

"What brings you here this morning?" she asked as her friend Beth poured herself a cup of coffee.

"The roofing crew is setting up out back."

Well, talk about unexpected news. "I didn't know that I'd hired a roofing crew."

"This company had two days of downtime they needed to fill and were willing to put a roof on for you for seven grand less than any of the other companies who bid it. I jumped at the deal before someone else could grab them. You, by the way, have a very easy signature to forge."

And her friend made it sound like such a good thing.

She'd been right; the trip to Kansas City was now out of the question. Timing-wise it was perfectly doable, but with a crew climbing around on her roof with buckets of hot tar… The roofers might have questions. There could be problems that she needed to be there to solve. Conscience-wise… No, as much as she wanted to, she just couldn't give herself permission to spend the entire day getting ready for a night with Cole Preston.

Five

Emily gritted her teeth, poured more of the chemical onto the rag, set the open can back on the kitchen counter and rubbed on the palm of her left hand some more. Of all the stupid things she'd ever done in her life… She paused to consider the coating of tar. Maybe, if she squinted, it looked like a little of it had come off. A glance at the rag said otherwise.

God, what was she going to do if she couldn't get the stuff off? She couldn't go anywhere in public all covered with tar. And she sure as hell couldn't go to dinner with Cole. No dress on earth was sexy enough to make a man blind to the fact that the woman wearing it had spent the day swimming in a tar pit. Fighting back a wave of desperation, she poured more of the solvent on the rag and and rubbed harder.

"Whoa, there."

Her stomach clenched and fell to the bottom of her feet. "Cole," she said flatly, lifting her gaze to where he stood in the open doorway of her apartment. "What are you doing here?"

Cole cocked a brow, but otherwise ignored her less than enthusiastic welcome. "I got bored watching computer screens," he answered, ambling toward her. "And I thought I'd come down and see if you needed help with anything."

She went back to scrubbing her hand. "I'm fine, thank you."

Yeah, he could see that. He could also smell the fumes. He glanced at the can on the counter. Ah, good ol' automotive chrome cleaner. The roofer's friend.

He leaned a hip against the edge of the kitchen counter and took in the extent of the damage she'd suffered. There was tar on her knees, her hands, even in her hair and on the curve of her left ear. He very causally tilted his head to change the angle of his view. Good Lord, the entire back side of her jeans was covered with the stuff.

He waited, but since she didn't volunteer an explanation for why she was standing in her kitchen, covered with tar and bathing in solvent... "Okay, I'll come right out and ask. Have you been rolling around on your new roof?"

She stopped scrubbing and her shoulders sagged as she sighed. "Well, if you must know," she replied, meeting his gaze. "In a moment of pure, unadulterated kindness, I took a plate of freshly baked chocolate chip cookies up to the guys working on the roof. While up there, in a moment of pure, unadulterated *grace,* I backed up, tripped over an empty tar bucket and landed flat on my fanny in front of God and the whole cookie-munching, horrified crew."

As he fought the urge to grin, she went on, "And while they speed-ate their cookies with one hand and held steaming tar mops with the other, I spent about ten of the longest, most humiliating moments of my recent life trying to get to my feet without making matters any worse than they already were."

He cleared his throat softly before he dared to observe, "I'm guessing, by the looks of you, that the effort wasn't terribly successful."

"Duh," she countered testily. "I'd only managed to get to my knees before one of them finally got a hand free and pulled me to my feet."

"Look on the bright side. You gave them a great story to tell in the bar tonight."

"Wonderful." She picked the can up from the counter and showed it to him, saying, "They told me this stuff would take the tar off. They didn't mention that I'd have to rub hard enough that it would take the first two layers of my skin with it."

"Would you like some help?" The look in her eyes was a fascinating mixture of mortification and resentment. "I spent the summer of my freshman year in college working construction," he hastily explained. "I actually have some experience at getting the stuff off fairly easily and without sacrificing too much of your hide."

"How?" she asked instantly. Okay, it was a bit warily, but at least her eyes weren't shooting daggers at him anymore.

"You start with a good, long, hot shower. The heat softens the tar, washing away some of it and making it easier for the solvent to do its thing on what's left. You go hop in, get it pliable and I'll take it from there."

She lowered her chin as she raised a brow.

"What?" he asked, recognizing a challenge when he saw one. "It really works. I wouldn't lie to you."

She picked up the can of solvent and walked off toward her bedroom saying crisply as she went, "I am not sharing a shower with you, Cole Preston. You are not going to see me naked."

Frowning, he watched her disappear. He wasn't going to see her naked? How in the hell had they come to this point? He thought back, step by step. He'd come over that morning. They'd headed over to Grams's for some privacy. The elevator fantasy had come up on the way out of the warehouse. Once at Grams's… They'd have been naked within minutes if Grams and the bridge ladies hadn't shown up. And then Emily had set up a dinner date slash elevator rendezvous on her way out.

And now she wasn't going to let him see her naked? Shaking his head, he went after her.

The bathroom was off on the right side of the

bedroom, directly opposite the foot of her bed. There wasn't a door. But there was a shower-tub combination with a definitely non see-through curtain. Her jeans and shirt lay in a stained heap on the floor beside the tub.

"Okay, I'm officially confused," he announced, stepping into the doorway just as a pair of panties appeared from behind one edge of the curtain and were dropped onto the pile.

She turned the faucet on full blast while saying, "Pretend there's a door there."

Cole snorted. As if she was going to come out of there after him if he crossed the line. He walked in, closed the lid on the toilet and made himself comfortable. Over the groaning of the pipes and the roar of the showerhead coming to life, he asked, "Correct me if I'm wrong, but I'm under the impression that we have a date for a fantasy elevator ride tonight."

"We do. After dinner at Vito's."

Well, she hadn't hesitated in answering and she certainly sounded like she might be looking forward to it. "Did I miss a memo or something? Is the evening over after the elevator ride?"

"I sincerely hope not."

Again, no hesitation and what sounded like anticipation. Which really didn't do a damned thing to clear up his confusion. "Well then, won't I see you naked at some point tonight?"

"That's tonight," she replied. "This is the afternoon."

If she thought that made any sense at all to him… "What difference does it make?"

"It makes a difference. A huge one."

So she said. Not that he could see it for the life of him. He fell back on the only explanation men had for such mysteries. "Is this one of those deals where it's some official Girl Rule that us guys have no clue about?"

"Yes."

The strangled sound of her reply… The odds were she wasn't drowning. "Are you crying in there?"

"No."

For God's sake. Tears over a little tar? "What are you crying about, Emily?"

It took a few moments, but she finally answered, her voice thick with tears and frustration, "This is *not* how it's supposed to go."

Cole closed his eyes and scrubbed his hands over his face. Part of him wanted to offer a few curt suggestions about putting things in perspective. The greater part of him, though, the insensitive part that was probably a genetic holdover from the Neanderthal age, wanted to laugh.

"Okay," he said, trying to take the middle ground, "take a deep breath, let the water run over your head for a minute and then kindly tell me what's not supposed to be whatever way that's upsetting you to the point of not crying."

Emily stood under the hot water, letting it sluice down over her body, and turned his words over in her mind. His request was convoluted, but she knew what he was asking. She was tempted to tell him that it was all beyond description, but that wouldn't have been honest.

Swiping away her tears, she sniffled and began, "I was going to go up to Kansas City this afternoon and do a whole day spa thing. Get a manicure and a pedicure and waxed and buffed and tanned so that…" Okay, there was such a thing as *too* honest. She sighed hard and long. "But, oh no, I decided that I needed to be responsible and stay here in case there was a problem with the roof."

"Being responsible is good, Emily."

"Yeah, right," she countered. "And now I'm standing in a hot shower trying to melt the tar off my body while you sit on my commode offering me words of encouragement and reassurance, and to scrub what I can't reach. This is *not* part of the elevator fantasy."

"Well, no," he quickly and brightly agreed. "The elevator fantasy begins when the elevator doors close and ends when they open."

He didn't get it. "You were supposed to think of me all day, envisioning me in a hot dress," she explained. "You weren't supposed to see me until I walked into Vito's tonight and blew your socks off. And now it's all ruined. The illusion has been shattered."

He didn't say anything, at least not that she could hear over the sound of the chugging plumbing and the running water. Stepping out from under the showerhead, she listened. And heard a low, rumbling, almost choking noise that sounded a lot like… "Are you laughing?" she asked.

"No. Absolutely not," he said, obviously lying through his teeth. "In fact, I'm thinking about crying, too."

"It's not funny, Cole."

He cleared his throat and had managed to control his outright laughter when he asked, "Would you like for me to go away? I will if you want me to."

"As if that would make any difference at this point," she countered, stepping back under the heated stream of water. "As if you could pretend you never saw me like this. You couldn't even pretend there was a bathroom door!"

"Emily, darlin'," he replied, his voice rippling with both amusement and patience. "I'm a guy. Reality doesn't ever get in the way of our fantasies. My socks are still going to get blown off tonight when you walk into Vito's."

Surprisingly, she believed him. Emily smiled and, because she didn't want him to think she'd surrendered too easily, observed, "It just won't be the same as it could have been."

Despite knowing that she couldn't see him, Cole grinned and held up his hand. "I swear to you that the wonder will be the same for me tonight. Nothing has been ruined at all."

The edge of the shower curtain drew back just enough for her to look out out at him. Her skin pinkened from the heat of the water, her hair a mass of wet curls around her face, she smiled sheepishly and said, "If you'd be so kind as to hand me the can of tar and bug remover from the top of the tank behind you."

He stood, picked up the can and then took the single step to stand right next to the tub. "Do you have any idea of just how adorable you are right this minute?"

The tips of her beautiful, deliciously soft lips curved up into the smallest, shyest smile. "Cole…"

His gaze fixed on hers, he blindly passed the can of solvent to her, murmuring, "Sugar and spice. Everything naughty and nice."

He slowly trailed a fingertip through the droplets along the length of her nose, then down to those luscious, tempting lips. She ever so slightly kissed his fingertip, sending a jolt of pure, demanding desire shooting to the center of his bones. If he stayed one second longer…

"See you tonight," he said softly, dropping his hand and backing away. "I'll be the guy with his jaw on the table."

Emily nodded. Or at least she thought she did. All she really knew for certain as she watched him leave was that somehow he had made her forget all about the disasters and disappointments of her day and made her feel special. And that made him something very special.

Cole rubbed the towel over his head, tossed it on the end of his bed and then tightened the sash of his bathrobe as he headed for the closet. Out of the corner of his eye, he saw his grandmother heading down the hall toward her own room. "Hi, Grams," he called. "What are your plans for the evening?"

She came back to stand in his doorway and answer, "I'm going to a nine-pin tap tournament at the bowling alley."

He froze, his suit halfway out of the closet. "Excuse me?" he asked, turning his head to look at her.

"Oh, for heaven's sake, I'm not bowling," she assured him, laughing. "I'm going for the front-row seat to watch Edgar Moore bowl."

"Is he that good?" he asked as he resumed his routine.

"I have no idea. But I do know that he's the only man over sixty in town who's still packing a fanny in his pants. The rest of them are as flat as boards back there."

"Grams!"

"Oh, he's married to Edith," she said with a dismissive flutter of her elegant hand. "And besides, that whole ear hair thing of his…" She shuddered and then smiled to add, "I may be old, Cole, but I am a long way from desperate. And there are certainly limits to my selective blindness. Do you need me to press your shirt?"

"It should be fine, Grams," he assured her as he laid his clothing on the bed. "But thanks for offering."

"I'm so glad that you and Emily have resolved your differences. You two look very cute together, you know. I hope you have a wonderful evening out. I'll leave the light on for you, but I hope you don't feel an obligation to be in by any certain time. I'm not going to wait up for you."

Well, as blessings went, that was as good as roundabout ones came. "Thanks, Grams," he called after her.

It was nice to know that his grandmother approved of—

Part of his brain running ninety to nothing and the other part of it sitting at a dead, totally numbed stop,

Cole dropped down on the side of the bed. How could he have… Damn, she was… Of all the… Not that he had… Maybe it really…

He pressed his hands into the sides of his head and squeezed, desperately trying to get his thoughts to slow down just enough to actually finish one. With a deep breath, he got to his feet.

He began to pace his bedroom, sorting the random stream of his thoughts into neat little mental categories. And when the last of them had been grasped and organized, he sat back down on the bed and logically went through them, analyzing each in turn.

Why was he in a bedroom at his grandmother's house in a town that wasn't anything more than a bump in the road? Because he'd been so alarmed at Grams's request to liquidate part of her portfolio to fund a new friend's community project that he'd slammed the brakes on his own life, jumped in the car and driven here to put things right.

And what had he discovered when he arrived here? A gorgeous, perky blonde with long legs, perfectly shaped breasts and an apparent willingness to turn his every fantasy into reality.

Emily was all that and intelligent, funny and delightful, too. He couldn't deny that and wouldn't even try.

And therein laid the problem. That was all he'd been aware of for the last… He tried to think back and coordinate the moments of the calendar. "Well, for however long," he muttered. "Doesn't really matter, anyway."

What mattered was that he'd completely lost track

of why he'd come to Augsburg, what his suspicions were, and the plan he'd had as he'd walked across the library lawn, stuck out his hand and made a truce with the green-eyed devilette.

Cole frowned at the floor between his bare feet. Actually, now that he thought about it, his plan to keep Emily Raines close so that she couldn't pull a con on Grams—or any other gullible old person for that matter—was working perfectly. So well, in fact, that he'd forgotten that it was a deliberate plan. But since it seemed to be working even better than he'd hoped… Okay, no harm, no foul. He didn't have a thing to be worried about on that front. As long as he remembered from time to time that it was a carefully calculated strategy, of course.

Now, as for the other issues that he needed to be concerned about… What to do about Grams was the most important. He couldn't spend the rest of his life in Augsburg. Well, he could, what with computers and high-speed Internet and all, but it made for a long drive to the airport where his plane was parked. And he wasn't likely to get any work done as long as Emily was anywhere around.

He cocked a brow. He was assuming that the fling with Emily wouldn't fizzle out by the end of the week. Since he knew himself and the way affairs typically went, the assumption was based on shaky ground.

Once a physical relationship was taken out of the equation, the situation changed considerably. He was right back to where he'd been when he'd turned off the highway and rolled into town. Grams was a soft touch for every cause that came down the pike with a sob story or a slick brochure. He didn't have the kind of life that would let him watch her every move every single second of the day.

And Emily Raines... While Jason's comprehensive investigation had turned up nothing and his own instincts said that she wasn't a con artist, that her motives were sincere and aboveboard, the logical part of him was tallying up some interesting observations. The fifty grand from a Secret Santa was a great story, but so good it was slightly suspect. And while, technically, he hadn't handed her so much as one real red cent, he was running an aggressive brokerage account for her with his money. In fairness, though, he had freely offered his expertise.

"And not exactly for free," he admitted, smiling and checking his watch.

A half hour would be plenty of time to do a quick, basic Internet search on elder care and get a general idea of what the range of options were. Narrowing them down to two or three should be fairly easy; most choices, even the hard ones, usually came down to a very limited number.

And if he did all that before he headed off to Vito's Italian Gardens, it would give him something to think about while he waited for Emily to arrive. And Lord knew he was going to need a handy mental distraction if she showed up looking even half as delicious as he was imagining.

Cole studied the two sheets of paper on the linen-covered table before him and took another sip of wine. Having narrowed the options down to two hadn't made the choice a slam dunk. Not by any means. One place, in Florida, looked a lot like a cruise ship on land. Twelve dining rooms, an activity staff of twenty, an on-site state-of-the-art medical facility and a campus that was nothing short of palatial. The price per month was palatial, too, but that wasn't his concern. The cost wasn't even a minor factor. Grams being happy there was, though, and he was having a hard time trying to mesh what Emily had said about the elderly needing to have their worlds small with the obvious massive, sprawling size of the Florida retirement complex.

The second option met the small requirement very easily. It was in Sedona and offered a spalike existence to no more than eight residents at any one time. Private chefs, physical therapists, a medical team on-site twenty-four-seven... He read the description again. No mention of planned activities for the clients. Well, that was a strike against it. The cost was right in line with the Florida facility, so the question boiled down to whether his grandmother would be comfortable there.

Huge, active and palatial versus small, personal and luxurious. The choice was Grams's, of course, but he really wanted to have a choice made in his own mind before he presented the whole idea to her.

His waiter appeared at the edge of the table. "Pardon the intrusion, sir. You asked to be told when your dinner companion arrived."

"Thank you," Cole replied, folding the papers and hastily tucking them into the inside pocket of his suit jacket. He slid out of the booth and stepped out from behind the foliage to watch Emily make her way toward him down the center aisle of the restaurant. She smiled as she saw him, her happiness and confidence every bit as sparkling as the crystals that surrounded the edges of what had to be the deepest plunging neckline he'd ever seen off the beach. One hooked finger and a little bit of a tug and he could kiss her navel.

As she'd promised, the dress was green and it was a halter type. He couldn't tell at the distance how easy the halter would be to undo, but undoing it wasn't going to a major factor. There wasn't all that much fabric there. All he had to do was slip his hands in under the crystal edge, push it aside and he'd be in heaven. His gaze traveled lower.

Her skirt wasn't as short or as tight as he'd expected, hitting her a few inches above the knee and skimming softly over her skin with every step she took, but he wasn't at all disappointed. No, his only regret as she reached his side and smiled up at him was the realization that if she hadn't been willing to make love with him with sparkies wandering around her place, it was a safe bet she wasn't going to be all that receptive to the idea of going for it on top of a table in a public restaurant.

"Good evening, Miss Raines," he said, bending down to brush a light kiss over her dark pink lips. "May I say how absolutely radiant you look this evening?"

"Thank you, Mr. Preston. You look quite handsome yourself."

"I'm afraid that all the tables were reserved when I called this afternoon. I hope a booth is all right?"

"It's perfect," she declared as she slid into the seat and slipped over to her place setting. "It's rather like being in a private little jungle all of our own," she added, looking around them. "Very nice. Very private."

"That crossed my mind, too," he supplied as he slid in beside her. "I took the liberty of ordering our wine."

"Have you thought of everything?"

"I sure hope so." He lifted his glass to her. "To adventure."

She tapped her rim ever so lightly against his. "With a bit of danger."

Yes, and speaking of danger… "How are the sparkies doing over at your place? All done?"

"They were cleaning and packing up as I left. Which is why I opted to wear the overskirt. I didn't want to give any of them whiplash."

"Overskirt?" The just above the knee thing wasn't the real skirt?

"It's kind of like a bathing suit cover," she explained. "It wraps around and hooks at the waist to give the appearance of a bit of modesty when one's out in a very public place."

"What's underneath?"

Her grin was delightfully wicked. "A very short, very well-fitted skirt that very eloquently says that going out in public was never so much as a minor, fleeting consideration." She paused for a second and then asked, "Would you like a peek?"

"No." She blinked at him, clearly stunned. He leaned close and whispered, "I want the whole reveal deal."

Her gaze darted to the world outside their sheltered enclave even as she reached for the front of the skirt's narrow waistband. Pooling the overskirt on either side of her on the seat, she leaned back, shifted slightly and crossed her long, lean legs.

Sweet Jesus. She hadn't been kidding about how short the skirt was or how well it fit her body. His blood heated. His jaw must have dropped, too, because she laughed softly and reached for her wineglass.

"So how is my stock portfolio doing this evening?" she asked after taking a sip.

"None of the trading triggers have activated yet," he explained, grateful to her for providing a much-needed momentary distraction. "A couple of them came close this afternoon, but didn't hit the magic number. You're still at your initial investment."

"Bummer."

Her little sigh of disappointment... He couldn't tell if she was seriously disappointed, or if she was simply continuing the bantering and teasing game they'd been playing over the matter of his management fees. "A lot can happen in overnight trading," he assured her. "You could wake up tomorrow morning the richest woman in Augsburg."

Her smile was absolutely, adorably wicked. The delightful sparkle in her eyes as she met his gaze sent his heartbeat into overdrive.

"Rich certainly isn't necessary," she said. "But it would be a nice bonus."

He laughed outright, delighted with her and with

himself for having had the good fortune of meeting her. Actually, now that he thought about it, he was delighted with the way life was going in every single respect.

With a little wink, she picked up the oversize menu, saying, "I'm not really very hungry, but we should probably look at the menu and order at least a little something."

"Agreed." He picked up his menu and opened it.

"What looks good to you?"

"You," he answered honestly from behind the restaurant's bill of fare. "That is some dress."

"Thank you. I was hoping you'd find it...inspirational."

"Inspirational is an understatement." Still holding his menu, he leaned over to whisper in her ear, "If I thought I could time the arrival of the waiter, I'd be licking my way up your thighs right this minute."

She didn't say a word, but her breath caught and her gaze, locked on the menu she held in front of her, went vacant. With a smile, he reached out and slowly, deliberately scraped the pad of his thumb over the hard bud pressing against the fabric of her bodice.

She blinked, drew a deep breath and shifted on the seat. "So tell me about some of the companies you've invested capital in," she said softly, angling her menu to block the access of his hand.

"Chicken," he laughingly countered as he settled back into his seat and quickly adjusted himself.

Ever so innocently, she said, "I had the chicken marsala the last time I ate here. It was good, but I think I want to try something different this time."

"Lasagna is usually a pretty safe bet."

"True, but it also tends to be heavy. I don't want to finish supper ready to take a nap."

"That would be a bummer."

"I think I'll have the shrimp scampi with the angel-hair pasta. What about you?"

He chuckled. "You can have me anytime you want. Just say the word, sweet Emily, and we're out of here."

She shot him a considerably less than dire warning look and laid aside her menu. "So tell me about some of the companies you invest in."

"Persistent little thing, aren't you?"

"I can be."

"I've noticed that. You have an exciting penchant for risk taking, too. I can't tell you how stimulating I find the combination."

Her gaze dropped to his lap, but even as she parted her perfectly pink lips to speak the waiter stepped through the opening in the foliage.

"Good evening, sir, ma'am," he said. "My name is Gino and I'll be your waiter this evening. Are you ready to order?"

Cole poured the last of the wine into their glasses and wondered exactly when and why his focus had become so damned one-tracked, how it was that she could sit there, her elbows on the table and her chin resting on her laced fingers while she asked him questions about his venture-capital projects, and he thought it was the sexiest dinner conversation he'd ever had.

"So," she said brightly, as the waiter silently cleared away their plates, "are you going to invest in the Louisiana Cane Conversion company?"

"I haven't decided yet," Cole admitted.

"What's the concern that's keeping you from making a commitment? Is it the technology?"

He shook his head. "No, that's been proven. LCC isn't reinventing the wheel. Their engineers have built a good dozen biorefineries in Brazil in just the last five years. They're considered to be the best."

"So why the holdback?"

"I'm not convinced that our government is willing to support anything other than corn as a source for biofuel production," he explained. "The corn belt has a well-organized, well-funded and laser-focused lobby working for their interests. The Louisiana sugar cane growers don't have any of that."

"But," she posed thoughtfully, "if you gamble on them and they actually make it as big as Brazil's growers have…"

"Move over Bill Gates, there's a new mega billionaire in town."

"Impressive," she allowed. "What's the price tag for the gamble?"

"Ten million in the initial funding outlay. More if it actually takes off."

"Can you afford to lose ten million?"

He chuckled ruefully and admitted, "I'm not a good sport when I lose a buck in a bad vending machine, so losing ten million of them would not make me happy. But, yes, I can afford the risk."

"Do I get to vote on it?"

"No," he said, already knowing what her vote would be. "Sorry."

"Well, I thought I'd give it a shot. I find all of this wheeling and dealing and future shaping…"

"A little like Greek?"

"It's way better than Greek." She sighed deeply and shifted on the seat. "Trust me."

"Oh, yeah?" he dared her. "How much better?"

He'd expected her to offer him another of her deliciously provocative innuendoes, not to silently take his lapels in her hands and deliberately draw his lips down to hers. Any thought of a waiter evaporated from his awareness as she traced the seam of his lips with the tip of her tongue. His awareness of place remained, but just barely. He opened his mouth for her and slipped his arms around her waist, drawing her closer so that she could more thoroughly wage her assault. In reward for his consideration, she eased her leg over his and sent his mind reeling.

The voice of restraint reminded him that they were in a restaurant. The voice of need pointed out that it was a long tablecloth. He slipped his hands down over the perfectly well-rounded curve of her rear, loving the way she moaned her approval into his mouth. With one hand he held her still while he slid the other down to the hem of her skirt and then around to the front and up beneath it.

As his fingers brushed over wet curls, she drew back

to meet his gaze and whisper, "I'm ready for dessert. How about you?"

He smiled, said, "Let me take care of the check and we'll be on our way," and eased her back onto the seat beside him. Taking a hundred-dollar bill from his wallet, he tossed it onto the table and then slid out to offer her his hand. She took it and allowed him to assist her to her feet. She reached back for her overskirt and held it up as though she intended to put it back on.

"Oh, I don't think so," Cole said, taking it from her hands.

She considered it for maybe half a second, then gave him a sultry smile and tiny shrug just before she slipped her arm around his and said, "Arguing would be such a waste of time."

With her overskirt draped over his forearm, Cole pulled the scissor door closed and stepped back against the elevator wall next to the control panel. Her smoldering emerald gaze boldly locked with his, Emily reached out blindly and punched the button for the second floor. The outer doors slid silently closed. As the car started upward, the corners of her mouth lifted in a wicked smile of expectation.

Far be it for him to disappoint her in any way. He punched the stop button, and as they gently lurched to a halt, dropped her skirt at their feet and reached for her, sliding his hands beneath the inside edges of her bodice and dragging his palms down over the firm mounds and hard peaks that had taunted him all through dinner.

She shuddered in delight as he cupped her fullness and scraped his thumbs slowly and firmly back and forth over her nipples.

Emily drew a deep breath as she savored the incredibly sweet aching his touch triggered in her breasts, the demanding heat he ignited deep in her core. There was no resisting the urge. No point in it, either. Not with the speed at which he was fanning her need. She ran her hands down his chest, caressing through his shirt the chiseled planes of heated flesh and hard muscle, and then moved lower, trailing her fingertips over the ripples of his abs. Reaching the waistband of his trousers, she said, "I hope you don't mind."

She already had his belt undone when he murmured, "Not at all," and abandoned her breasts to reach into his pants pocket. A second later he produced a small foil packet. As he tore it open, she undid his zipper.

"Shall I?" he asked. "Or do you want to?"

"You," she answered, pushing his pants and shirt out of their way. No underwear, bless him. "I'll help, though," she added, taking his hardened shaft in her hands. She heard him suck a hard breath through his teeth, heard it catch deep in the center of his chest as she drew her palms up the heated length of him.

As much as he hated having to interfere with her attentions, Cole couldn't risk letting her set the pace. What self-control he normally had had been largely shredded in the course of dinner. No way did he want to leave her frustrated and wanting. He gently but firmly pushed her hands away and rolled the condom on.

A wicked, appreciative smile tipped up the corners of her mouth as she looked up to meet his gaze. God, she was beautiful. Sexy beyond anything any man had ever seen in a magazine. She was real, flesh and blood, fiery desire and unstinted passion. And she was all his. He slipped his arms around her, cupped her bottom and drew her hard against the full length of his body.

Her arms twined around his neck, she tipped her head back and offered him her parted lips. She could feel the hammering beat of his heart everywhere their bodies touched, could feel her need curling low and building deep inside her. Her legs weakening, she melted into him as the heat in her core fanned out to fill every fiber of her body. God, she couldn't ever remember wanting so much this fast. If she didn't get control, didn't tamp her hunger down…

But even as the last remnant of rational thought was offering advice, she instinctively knew there was absolutely nothing she could do to alter the course or the pace. What was, was. All of her senses were intensely aware, so wondrously alive, there was no putting them in a bottle, no calling a time-out for a steadying breath.

Her breasts throbbed with sweet pleasure as she and Cole moved against each other. The heat and hardness of his erection pressed into her abdomen, taunting her, teasing her, feeding her hunger. She rose on her toes, pressing herself closer, tightening her arms around his neck, and deepened their kiss, wordlessly begging him to match the frantic pace of her spiraling need.

He moaned, low and deep in his chest, and scraped

his hands down the back of her thighs to the hem of her skirt. She whimpered in desperate approval, dragging her leg up the side of his as he pulled her skirt to her waist. She wanted to climb, needed to climb. *Now.*

His mind saturated with the feel of her hot, silken skin, Cole barely heard the word buried deep in the sound of her pleasure. But he did. And if she wanted *now*… God knew he'd wanted *now* since the doors had closed. He cupped her buttocks and lifted her up. She instantly wrapped her legs around his hips and he whirled about, pressing her hard against the elevator wall and bending his knees. She kissed him deeper, her quick, hard moans vibrating through him and urging him on, begging him for more, for faster. For *now.*

And he obliged her, obliged himself, driving upward and burying himself deep within the throbbing heat of her need. She drew her head back and gasped for air, her gaze locked with his, silently commanding. He smiled and drew back slightly, then drove into her again, filling her, hard and fast.

"More. God, more," she moaned, her eyelids drifting down. He drew back and thrust again, and again. "Yes," she whimpered as he set the rhythm of his strokes. "Don't stop, Cole."

Her senses reeling and awash with pure, pulsing pleasure, she clung to him and rode the rocketing crest upward. Power and strength. Heat and hunger. All that was her world in this moment, all that she had ever wanted, all that she would ever need.

She cried out in relief and happiness as the bloom

of completion began to unfurl deep in her core. She arched back against the wall and pressed her hips against the power of Cole's magnificent body, demanding, begging that he understand how desperately she needed to reach the end.

And he heard her plea, shifting his hands to hold her hips tight and driving deep. The heavy coil of her need shattered in an explosion of utterly pure, exquisitely raw pleasure. She gasped in happiness and called out his name as wave after gloriously intense wave of body-wracking wonder and delight consumed her.

When the last one ebbed away, her soul was left quiet, and her mind calm enough to note more subtle sensations. She smiled. Cole. Slowly pressing soft little kisses to the side of her neck, his breathing every bit as ragged as hers was. She pried open her eyes and let the real, everyday details around her bring her mind back to center.

His body was relaxed against hers, the fierce driving tension that had been in all his muscles washed away. She sighed in contentment and thought about offering an apology for having been so wrapped up in her own moment of incredible pleasure that she'd missed his entirely. Moistening her parched lips with the tip of her tongue, she drew a steadying breath. Even as she did, his chest and shoulders began to gently shake.

Twining her fingers through the hair at the nape of his neck, she quietly asked, "Are you laughing or crying?"

He lifted his head from her shoulder to grin lazily at her. "Laughing. Sort of."

"Why?"

He leaned forward and bushed a light, butterfly kiss over her lips. "Because," he said as he drew back, "I'm so thoroughly drained and satisfied, I'm thinking I may not be able to move anytime real soon."

"I'm sorry I missed yours," she offered. "I was too busy selfishly enjoying my own to pay even the slightest bit of attention to anything else."

He chuckled and gave her an easy hug. "Well, if it makes you feel any better, I only caught the first few seconds of yours. And then I was off in my own world, too. Next time maybe we can take it a bit slower so we can properly savor each other's moment."

Well, that was good in theory. "I think it's only fair to mention that it may be a while before I can work up another want that intense. I've never been anywhere near this satisfied before."

"Oh, yeah?" He gave her another quick kiss. "I'm going to take that as a personal challenge, you know."

God love him. And more power to him. "Am I getting heavy?"

"Not really. I've got you fairly well pinned against the wall."

"Beautifully, I'd say. I have no complaints. I could stay like this for another lifetime or so." Even as she spoke, a warning twinge shot down her leg. "Well, okay, now that I think about it, my hips are getting a little stiff."

"All right," he offered, laughing. "Let me see if we can't get ourselves slightly less tangled without ending up in a heap on the floor."

He managed the task just fine, shifting his hold on her ever so slightly so that she could ease her legs down and put her feet under herself. The world swayed a bit as she took responsibility for her own balance, but he steadied her until everything came right.

And then with another quick, light kiss, he let her go and stepped away to deal with his own need to put himself back together. Her skirt pulled back down, she waited until he'd fastened the button on his waistband, and then hit the stop button to release the car.

As they eased upward, he smiled and opened his arms. She stepped into his embrace, tipped her head back for his kiss and let him fan her fires to life again.

Six

Life is good. Emily cradled her hands behind her head on the pillow, smiled up at the ceiling and listened to the shower run in the bathroom. If she had an ounce of energy left in her, she'd roll off the bed and have another turn at that fantasy, too. The first shower together had been when they'd first come into the apartment. The plan for going slow enough to savor each other's climax had… Emily chuckled softly. Gone down the drain.

Oh, well, it was impossible to be disappointed. Satisfied was satisfied. And fast and furious, part two, had been every bit as mind-blowingly wonderful as the elevator interlude. Maybe even better for her having had a sturdy towel bar to hang on to as Cole had held her hips in front of him and sent them both way over the moon.

They'd slept a bit after that, so spent that they'd awakened sprawled across the bed in each other's arms and still wrapped in damp towels.

Yep, life is good. And she'd never again look at a case of bed hair as an inherently bad thing. The quick wetting to put it back to a semblance of nonweird shape... Finally, slow and easy and savoring had been possible. And so well worth the attempt.

But like all good things... Emily sighed and rolled off the bed and onto her feet. Dawn had been hours ago and the world was calling them. The least she could do was gather up Cole's scattered clothes and have them ready for him when he got out of the shower. She pulled on her silk robe and while tying the sash, padded out into the living room.

She laughed at the trail that laid in a fairly direct line from the front door to the bedroom. If that didn't tell a story.... She bent down and picked up his socks, then retrieved his pants. His shirt was next in the line, only a few feet away from his tie. His shoes were next and last, just inside the front door was his jacket, laying right beside the green pool of her dress.

She picked up his jacket first and gave it a good shake, hoping that it would help to ease away come of wrinkles. A square of paper flipped out and landed on the floor with a hefty *whack.* Emily scooped it up, her gaze automatically skimming the words as she went to put it in one of his pockets. She stopped and read it more carefully.

Damn. Damn, damn, damn. It crossed her mind to

put it away and pretend that she'd never seen it, to act as though she didn't know—or care—what he was thinking and planning. But she did care. And while, no, it wasn't the way she had had in mind to end their night together, what would be the point of wandering over to Ida's later in the day and confessing to what she'd found hours earlier? She'd found it, she knew what it meant, and she needed to deal with it square up and straight on.

She took his clothes into the bedroom, gave them another shake and laid them out on the foot of the bed for him. The shower tap went off as she sat down on the corner of the mattress, unfolded the papers and gave them her first detailed inspection.

The Florida place looked like a cross between a casino and cruise ship. Glitz, glitter and a slick Web site presentation designed to impress. For four grand a month for the most basic package, she wasn't as impressed with the actual deal as she knew they wanted people to be.

The Sedona place… Why on earth did she have the feeling that the owners had tried and failed at running a posh dog kennel and were taking another run at making the ol' ranchero pay by pampering old folks instead of pooches? If they'd charged just under four grand a month for doggy retreats, it was no wonder they'd gone bust. She wouldn't hold out much hope for them being all that much more successful at housing people.

She stacked the two printouts, neatened the edges and refolded them into the neat little square that Cole had made of them. It was only after she'd finished the task that she realized that he'd come out of the bathroom. He stood in the doorway, a towel wrapped around his waist, another draped around his neck. He scraped his fingers through his tousled hair as he looked at the papers she still held in her hand.

She'd been caught. He'd been caught. There was no denying that they both knew what was hanging in the air between them.

Emily tossed the papers down on the bed. "This fell out of your jacket pocket when I was gathering up your clothes. Is it another venture-capital thing?" she asked lightly, hoping for an answer that would probably fall in the minor miracle category.

"You know that it's not," he said, crossing the room to stand by the end of the bed.

Part of her was glad he was being honest. Another part of her was sick at heart for what they stood to lose in locking horns over his grandmother's care. "What does Ida think about these places?"

He picked up his shirt, checked to make sure that she'd left him a few buttons and replied, "I haven't shared them with her yet."

"Smart choice," she observed dryly, arching a brow. "If I were you, I'd think real hard—a couple of times—before I brought up the idea of sending her off to pasture."

"These places can't be considered pastures in any way," he countered, tossing down the shirt and snatching up the papers. He opened the folds and held them out, one in each hand, as if she hadn't seen them before. "Not by a long stretch. They're incredibly nice. Didn't you read the details of what kind of services they offer to the residents?"

The insistent way he shook them at her... She took them with a silent sigh and prayer for patience. As she read over them a second time, he pulled on his shirt and fastened the only three remaining buttons on the front.

"Okay, there," she said, laying them on the bed in front of her as he noticed that a cuff button was missing, too. "I've read them. Now let me ask you, Cole... Why would you spend four thousand dollars a month for Ida to live in either one of these places when she can have very much the same thing for a whole lot less while living right where she is now?"

"You don't understand," he growled, rolling up his shirtsleeves.

"Obviously. Enlighten me."

"She's my grandmother. Not yours."

If he thought claiming proximity was going to be good enough to avoid making a case, he had another think coming. "Well, she's my friend and I'll bet you one sugar cane biofuel refinery that she would rather *die* than be shipped off to live in an old-folks home."

"These are hardly your typical old-folks homes."

She stopped herself from bluntly asking when he'd ever been in a retirement home and took a more indirect approach to make the point. "Oh, yeah? Do they have a preschool on-site? An after school latchkey program? Do the Girl Scouts make the rounds selling cookies? The

Cub Scouts their popcorn? Do the high school couples drop by to do a promenade of their rented tuxes and fancy gowns before the big night out? Do you see anyone in those pictures that's a day less than sixty-five?"

"They're *retirement* communities," he shot back, dropping down on the bed, his back to her, and yanking his pants on. "They're places where people go to live so they don't have to be guilt-tripped into buying cookies and popcorn they really don't want. Or put up with badly behaved toddlers and teenagers."

Yeah, that was the standard myth, the candle that drew the moths to the fatal flame. "That may be true in part. But mostly they're places, Cole," she said patiently, "where people go to quietly fade away and die without their families having to watch, feel guilty or be the least bit inconvenienced."

He stood, stripped away the towel and quickly pulled his trousers up around his waist. "They're places where the elderly are protected and safe."

"Protected from what?" He gave her a look that said she really shouldn't have had to ask. Well, she did, because she had no idea what he was talking about. "God, don't tell me you're one of those people who think that there's a serial killer lurking behind every bush waiting to jump out and hack granny to death when she goes to the mailbox for her Social Security check."

"Now you're being ridiculous."

"So answer the question," she challenged. "And answer it specifically. What is it that Ida needs to be protected from?"

He sat back down on the bed and picked up his socks. "Unrestricted access."

"What?" Emily asked, astounded. "You think she should be the human version of Area Fifty-One?"

His shoulders sagged and he heaved a sigh of surrender. "Grams is a notoriously soft touch," he said, slowly turning to face her. "You know all those solicitations that come in the mail every other day? The crippled children, the burned children, the third-world children, the orphans, the soldiers, the sailors, the missionaries, the dolphins, the whales, the caribou, the bison, the blind dogs, the tailless cats, the trees in Brazil, the ice in Antarctica, the—"

"I got it, Cole," she gently interrupted.

He shook his head. "You're on the go-to list for the Smithsonian when it comes to stained glass. Which is great. It's how you make a living. But my grandmother is on the go-to list for every lunatic and fringe cause known to mankind. They need money, they fire a set of address labels and a form letter out to Ida Bentley. Ida can be counted on to zip them a check the day she gets it."

He sighed and scraped his fingers through his hair again. "For God's sake, Emily, she's got a dozen shoe boxes in her bedroom closet right this minute, all of them stuffed full of fricking address labels."

"Not every charity is lunatic or on the fringe," she pointed out, trying to help him deal with a situation that had clearly frazzled his coping strategies.

"The point," he said crisply, sadly, "is that my grandmother doesn't make the distinction. Last year she bought six Holstein heifers for a village in Guatemala, eight pairs of rabbits for a village somewhere in India and paid for reconstructive surgery for three orphans with harelips somewhere in Lower Transylvania. Or maybe it was Upper, I don't know. I don't care. The important fact is that, altogether, it totaled close to fifteen grand."

"Was it money she didn't have?"

"She has the money," he assured her morosely.

"Then what exactly is the problem, Cole?" Emily pressed gently. "If it's her money, then she's entitled to spend it any way she wants. Clearly she thinks she's making a difference in the world when she writes a check. What's wrong with that? We all want to make the world better."

He gave her a tight smile. "Last year was also a group who wants to outlaw the internal combustion engine, the group who is publishing a dictionary of whale-speak, the group who blew up three family planning clinics, the—"

"I heard about that one," Emily admitted, suddenly understanding that his frustrations were based on a reality that had actually moved beyond eccentric and into dangerous.

"Yeah, well," he said, gaining his feet and beginning to pace, "Ida Bentley's generous contribution bought the dynamite." He threw his arms up and turned to her. "And let me tell you, you have not had a real nightmare until the FBI shows up on your doorstep asking questions about your grandmother's subversive activities."

"Okay, I understand your concerns," she allowed. "But why do you think moving Ida to some retirement village is going to change things? Do they restrict what mail the residents get?"

"I don't know." He came back to the bed and picked up his socks again. "It's one of the many questions I have to ask before I make any sort of decision."

"Well, if they can do that at those places, then it can be done right here, too. There's no need to ship Ida off into exile."

"It's not exile. These are extremely nice places."

"They're not real communities, either, Cole. My grandmother has gone before yours. I've been down this road. These places are really nothing more than very expensive, very profitable warehouses for old people on the end-of-life conveyor belt. You start in the independent living apartments, then you move over to the assisted living ones, then they roll you over to the nursing home, and then they load you in the wagon and haul you off to the morgue."

At least he seemed to be thinking about what she'd said. Either that or he was really having to concentrate on getting his socks and shoes on. "And the alternative?" he finally asked.

"You stay in your home, live your life as you always have, arrange for in-home living and nursing care when you need it, and when you have to have more intensive or specialized care than a visiting professional can provide… That's when you look at the nursing home. You don't climb on the conveyor belt before you absolutely have to. You sure don't do it so that your mail can be screened before you get it."

He stood, picked up the papers from the bed, folded them and then picked up his jacket to tuck them into the inside pocket. All without saying a word, without so much as a quick glance in her direction.

"Why don't you go talk to Jay, the postmaster here in Augsburg," she suggested kindly, "and see what you can do about controlling the solicitations?"

He nodded and then slowly looked up from his jacket to meet her gaze. "Who do I see, Emily, about controlling the appeals and pitches made twenty times an hour on every single TV station out there, twenty-four-seven? And who do I see about keeping the fraudulent contractors from knocking on her door and asking to fix her roof or trim her trees or clean her gutters or paint her house?"

"Maybe it's time for Ida to let someone else handle all the hassles of keeping a checkbook."

"You think?"

She ignored his sarcasm and countered with deliberate optimism, "Which is quite doable without upending her whole world by sending her off to live in a swamp or a desert."

"But that's based on the assumption that she'd agree to go along with it. I don't think she would."

Good God, if he thought she'd fight him over giving up control of a checkbook, had he really given any thought at all as to what her reaction would be to the notion that she move into a home? He wasn't just frazzled over the whole thing, his brain was fried.

"Then you just have to figure out some way to

restrict her access to checks," she offered diplomatically, climbing off the bed. "And debit and credit cards, too, I suppose."

Again he gave her a tight smile. "She used a credit card to donate the dynamite money. It took the FBI all of five seconds to come up with her name and maybe ten minutes for the credit card company to give them mine. There's now a flag on all of her cards that goes up when someone off the standard retail and golden charity list sends through a request for payment. And the credit agencies have flagged her reports to let me know if she applies for new cards."

"Well, you obviously have that under good control. I assume that you've enrolled her in one of those identity protection services, too?"

"Yes."

She walked to the end of the bed and slipped her arms around his waist. "You're a good man, Cole Preston," she assured him as she smiled up at him.

He put his arms around her and managed a close imitation of a genuine smile. "I'm a hard-hearted bastard who wants to ship his grandmother off to a plush prison, remember?"

"Yes, but I'm sure that, in the end, you'll consider all the options and choose the one that's best for her. You would never do anything that you know would make her unhappy. If there's anything I can do to help, all you have to do is ask."

"Which job do you want? Tripping the mailman, or grabbing the mail sack?"

She grinned. "Both are federal offenses. I'm pretty sure we can think of a solution that isn't going to land us in Leavenworth."

"At least the FBI would know where to find me when the Japanese Prime Minister gets *harpooned* by Greenpeace."

She laughed and hugged him. "Life has a way of working out like it should, Cole. There's no point in borrowing trouble in advance. When it's time to really deal with caring for Ida, you'll know exactly what the right decision is. Today isn't the day."

"You're sure of that?"

"Absolutely."

"Thanks, Emily," he whispered, lowering his mouth to hers.

"Yoo-hoo! Emily! Are you in here?"

He jerked back and cocked a brow. They both looked toward the front door at the same time to find her friend Beth standing just inside the apartment, holding the green dress at arm's length and blinking furiously.

"The party's over," Emily said, taking her arms from around him with a regretful smile. "I'll introduce you on your way out."

"Oh, damn, Em," Beth gushed as they came out of the bedroom together. "I'm so sorry. I didn't know. Didn't even suspect!"

"It's okay," Emily assured her.

"Yeah," Cole added. "Although it would be a different story if we'd still been hanging from the chandelier."

Beth's gaze instantly went to the ceiling, to the simple glass cover over the single light bulb.

"He's kidding," Emily assured her friend. "Beth, meet Cole Preston, Ida Bentley's grandson. Cole, my friend Beth Hardesty, the CPA and very literal thinker."

Cole stepped forward and with a grin, stuck out his hand and said, "Nice to meet you, Beth."

"Me, too," she stammered. "I really hope I'm not interrupting anything."

"Not at all," he said, giving Emily a quick kiss on the cheek. "Life is just working out the way it should. See you tonight?"

Her heart swelling, she nodded. "I'll be here."

"Have a good one," he called over his shoulder as he walked out of the apartment, his jacket slung over his shoulder. "Don't mug any mailmen without me!"

Emily laughed, watched him get on the elevator, and waved goodbye as the doors closed.

"Mailmen?"

"It would take too long to explain it," Emily replied, closing the apartment door and taking her dress from her friend's hand. "I should probably get dressed."

Beth nodded and headed into the kitchen, saying, "Yeah, I don't think Augsburg is quite ready to consider a peekaboo peignoir acceptable day wear."

"It's not peekaboo," Emily retorted, moving off toward the bedroom, checking the fabric of her sleeve just to make sure.

"Reach for something and it is," Beth called, getting a chunk of cheese out of the refrigerator. "Amazing how much so little fabric can cost, huh? Was he worth it?"

"Oh...my...God," Emily replied, pausing in the bedroom doorway.

"Don't tell me any more," Beth groused as she got a knife from the drawer. "I'd have to slit my wrists."

Emily went into the bedroom, grinning and feeling more alive than she could ever remember. Gathering up Cole's damp towels, she found his tie lying forgotten in the twisted sheets. She picked it up, too, and breathed deep the heady scent of his cologne. Oh, yes, he was most definitely worth a whole new lingerie wardrobe.

Maybe she should just accidentally leave a catalog on the coffee table before he came over this evening. Discussing possible purchases would be an easy, nonthreatening way to get an idea of just how long he intended to be around. If he was a one-week wonder, she could save her money. But if he wasn't making any plans to head for the hills anytime soon, well, then it was Katy bar—

Emily stopped, took a slow, deep breath and lifted her chin. They'd had one night together. A fabulous night, yes, but it wasn't the stuff on which a smart woman built a whole new wardrobe. Not even for a week of fun and breathless games. And she sure as hell didn't have any business even vaguely hoping that blow-the-top-of-your-head-off-curl-your-toes sex would bloom into a long-term relationship they could take outside the bedroom.

"Scratch the catalog idea," she muttered to herself as she opened a dresser drawer and collected her clothes. "Just play it as it goes and don't get greedy."

* * *

He'd managed to remember, of all things, most of the words to the song "Zip-A-Dee-Doo-Dah" by the time he bounded up the front walk of his grandmother's house. A blast from the past, of days of his childhood spent sprawled on the floor of the living room of Grams's Manhattan forty-second-floor condo, watching videotapes of old Disney movies. Damn, if he couldn't still see and hear Uncle Remus and the pudgy-faced bluebirds.

"It *is* a wonderful day," he said as he let himself into the house.

"Hello, dear!" his grandmother called from the dining room.

"Hi," he said in greeting, hanging his jacket on the back of a chair as he noted that she was sorting papers on the table. There were three stacks of brand-new address labels. "I see the mail's come already today."

"With lots of goodies in it," she answered happily. She handed him a small rectangular cedar box, stamped on the top with the name of a Native American tribe he'd never heard of. He opened the lid and found it neatly packed with pencils, also made of cedar and stamped with the name of the tribe.

"This was a gift, I presume?"

"Last month I sent them thirty dollars for vocational development programs."

Cole expelled a long, slow breath and considered the box of pencils in his hand. "You could have bought these at an office supply store for less than a buck."

"The ones at the store aren't made of cedar," she

countered, still sorting her mail. "Nor are they stamped with the tribal logo."

"That's really beside the point, don't you think?"

She stopped sorting and looked up to meet his gaze. "No, Cole, I think it's the whole point. Pencils bought at the store don't help anyone except the importer and the retailer. These go toward helping minority, disadvantaged young men and women learn a lifelong trade."

Yeah, there was a lot of demand for traditional number-two lead pencil makers these days. "Okay," he said, choosing to avoid the fight. "Point taken and accepted. More address labels?" He mentally kicked himself the second the words left his tongue.

"Are you planning to give me another of your lectures about charitable responsibility?" Grams asked crisply. "I have apologized I don't know how many times for that whole clinic bombing thing. I had no idea that was the sort of people they were, and I truly believed that I was funding the purchase of bassinets and receiving blankets."

He held up his hands in surrender. "No lecture, Grams. I promise."

"Thank you." She smiled and her blue eyes twinkled. "How was your dinner last night?"

Uh-oh. The Grilling. "Fine," he answered vaguely, knowing that she wasn't going to let him get away it.

"What did you have to eat?"

Damn, what a time for his brain to replay the image of Emily coming toward him in that killer dress of hers.

"You did go to dinner, didn't you?"

"Well, yes. I just don't..." *Make something up,* suggested a disgusted voice in the back of his brain. "Veal Parmesan. It was very good."

"And did Emily enjoy her meal, too?"

"She said she did."

"And how is she this morning?"

Oh, that was a new level for The Grilling. "I don't know," he replied with a cavalier shrug. Grams's brows slowly rose. "Well, you see, Grams," he said, "there was this really hot chick tending the bar named Bambi and—"

"Cole Edward Preston!"

"Emily is fine," he laughingly supplied. "And that's all I'm going to tell you."

"Are you seeing her again tonight?"

"She has a roofing crew going to work this morning. I don't know if she'll be able to get away this evening, or if the whole construction deal will leave her too exhausted to do anything but fall down and go to sleep. I'm going to play it by ear."

She nodded slowly, the way she used to when he maintained that he hadn't eaten the last six truffles in the box when they both knew he'd been the only one in the house. "Speaking of sleep, you look like you could use a good nap."

"Nice try, Grams," he said, grinning. "I'm going to go fix myself some toast. Would you like some?"

"Thank you, but no thank you. I had breakfast hours ago."

"Hours ago" implying, he knew, that he had obviously been too otherwise engaged to think about breakfast until now. He didn't say anything, though, just smiled pleasantly and left her to her sorting.

He was smearing peanut butter on his third slice of wheat toast when the swinging door from the dining room smacked against the kitchen counter. His grandmother strode in a half second later.

"Cole?"

"Yes, ma'am?" he replied, his mind whirling through the list of his recent sins and how many she might know about.

She threw a familiar folded square of paper down on the counter beside the butter dish. "I am *not* going to a retirement home. Any*where.* At *any* time. I am staying in this house until Mr. Baker comes to haul me over to the funeral home."

He looked at the paper. "You went through my pockets?" was the only thing he could think to say.

"I was going to press the wrinkles out of your jacket."

Women and their damn war against wrinkles. This was twice inside of a single hour! "I think," he began, trying to think diplomatically, "it's something we should talk about, Grams. Not necessarily now, but sometime down the road. You're not always going to be able to—"

"You are *quite* welcome to have the conversation anytime you like, Cole. Do *not,* however, expect me to participate. I have made the last move of my life. I'm not leaving here unless it's on a gurney, feetfirst and cutting a *lovely* feminine figure under a blue velvet Baker Funeral Home cover."

And with that declaration, she turned around and stomped out of the kitchen. He took a bite of his toast and slowly chewed, pondering what appeared to be a universal female aversion to the whole concept of retirement living. Was it some sort of hormonal aversion to golfing and shuffleboard, to day trips on little buses with chirpy, cheerful activity directors? Okay, he could see that the day trip thing might wear real thin real fast, but… Hell, they could call a taxi and flip the activity director off as they rolled down the driveway and past the little bus.

Was there something about community dining rooms that they simply couldn't bear to think about? Or was it that there were, on average, ten females for every male in typical retirement communities and they didn't want to have to spend their last years in constant catfights? Not that he could picture Grams doing anything other than regally holding court at which all the men kneeled at her feet and begged for her favor.

Whatever the reason for their visceral aversion… Cole picked up the printouts his grandmother had tossed on the counter, then walked over to the back door and dropped them into the trash can.

"There," he said around another bite of toast. "Never to be mentioned again." He should have listened to Emily and thrown it away while he was at her place. Emily really did have a good handle on life and people.

Considering the whole matter resolved, he finished his toast, cleaned up the kitchen and then headed upstairs for a well-deserved nap. Odds were, after all, that Emily wasn't going to be hauling buckets of hot tar around her roof all day and wouldn't be dead tired by dinnertime. He'd pick up some deli sandwiches on his way over and maybe a six-pack of some good imported beer. They could have a quiet evening in together, curled up together on the sofa talking about… Cole grinned. Futures markets and commodity exchanges, international currency trading and the valuation of the Chinese yuan. She'd be putty in his hands.

Cole frowned. Private beach in Hawaii, palm trees and waves, Emily wearing nothing but a lei. Why was there suddenly a gushing, sloppy slurry operation in his dream paradise?

"Shole?"

There it was again.

"Shole? Wase up, pease."

Someone was shaking his shoulder. He pried his eyes open and struggled to focus his vision on reality. His grandmother sat on the edge of his bed, her one hand on his shoulder, the other dangling from an arm hanging limply at her side. His heart shot instantly into his throat. He sat up and took her hand in his. "What is it, Grams?"

"Somesings…" She sucked a wet, slurpy breath. A thin line of saliva trickled from the corner of her mouth.

"Smile for me," he commanded even as he was yanking his cell phone out of its holster on his hip. She tried, but as he had known would happen, only one side of her face lifted for the effort.

"Nine-one-one," said the dispatcher on the other end of the phone connection.

He didn't wait for her to ask what his emergency might be, he barked out the address, his grandmother's name and age, and choked back a sob as he uttered the dreaded, horrible word *stroke*.

Seven

Emily slammed the car door behind her and sprinted across the hospital parking lot, her car keys gripped tight in one hand, her purse strap in the other. The extra-wide emergency entrance doors opened to let an ambulance crew roll their empty gurney back to their wagon and Emily shot past them, slowing down once inside only long enough to get a bead on the reception desk.

She slid to a halt in front of it and gasped, "Ida Bentley."

The woman on the other side of the counter considered her for a long second and then slowly swiveled all of ten degrees in her chair to look down a list of names on her computer screen. Turning back the ten degrees, she folded her hands on her desk and said, "She's back in the examining room. If—"

"Which one?" Emily demanded, her gaze darting around in search of doors with numbers on them.

"Only immediate family may go back with the patient."

"I'm family," she said, the lie tumbling off her tongue without so much as a moment's hesitation. "She's my grandmother-in-law."

Ten degrees to the computer screen… "Your name?"

"Emily Preston," she supplied. "Her grandson Cole is my husband. We're her only living relatives. I was told that he came here in the ambulance with her."

Ten degrees back… She inclined her head ever so slightly toward a set of wooden doors on Emily's right and then absently pushed a red button on the desk top, saying, "Room three, second on the left."

"Thanks!"

The big doors whooshed open and she shot through the opening, turned to the left and came to another skidding stop before the open door of Exam Room 3. There wasn't any hospital bed in it, just the empty space where it was obviously supposed to be. Cole sat in a blue plastic chair against the far wall, his elbows on his knees, his face buried in his hands.

She paused, expelled a breath in a long, slow stream and then took two deep ones to calm herself before she called softly, "Cole?"

He whipped his head up as though he'd been shot. His eyes were red-rimmed and his dark lashes clumped from his tears. He swallowed, quickly scraped the heels of his hands across his eyes and then met her gaze again.

"Where's Ida?"

"They're doing a CAT scan," he said, pushing himself slowly to his feet.

"What happened?" Emily asked, tossing her purse down on another chair and crossing the room. "Did she fall?"

He opened his arms for her and she stepped into his embrace, wrapping her arms around his waist as he answered, "She's had a stroke."

Her cheek pressed against the warmth of his chest, she heard and felt the hard, rapid beat of his heart. "Do they know what kind yet?" she asked, beginning to gather the information she needed in order to help him get through the ordeal. "Did they give you any idea of how severe they think it is?"

"I don't know anything, Emily," he answered, his voice tight, his arms around her even tighter. "Not one damned thing."

All right, it was time to get him focused and thinking. Enough of the being passive and wallowing in his understandable, but pointless, misery. Staying within his embrace, she eased back far enough that she could meet his gaze again. "What did Tim and Larry tell you?"

His brows knit as he thought back. "Who?"

"Tim and Larry are Augsburg's EMTs, the first responders that came to the house and brought Ida over here. Did they say anything?"

He eased his arms from around her and began to slowly pace. "Okay, let's see," he began. "They got there, checked Grams out, asked me when the symptoms began and then put her on a gurney. I couldn't really tell them anything for sure, Emily. Grams was fine when I came in this morning and then she woke me up, slurring her speech and drooling, one side of her body just limp."

"Were you able to give them a best guess for a time between fine and slurring?"

"I said two hours maybe. But I honestly don't know. I didn't look at a clock before I fell down on the bed."

She was running her morning against the clock, ticking off the minutes in her mind to see if she could get a better idea of how long it had taken to get Ida help when Cole said, his voice tighter than before, "God, Emily, I don't know how she got to my room in that condition. She had to have dragged herself down… God, I'm the world's worst excuse for a grandson."

"Cole," she said firmly, stepping into his path in an effort to force him to pay attention, "it's not your fault that Ida's had a stroke."

"Oh, yeah? Wanna bet?"

Seeing that neither simple assertion nor logic were going to work, she opted for the ridiculous. "You didn't throw away her boxes of address labels, did you?"

He gave her a smile. A real one. It lasted for only a second. "She found the retirement home stuff in my jacket pocket and she was not happy about it. Her blood pressure probably went through the roof." He dragged his fingers through his hair. "Jesus. You warned me and I didn't listen."

"Unless you charged up the stairs," she countered, continuing her course, "pulled out her suitcases and started packing for her, I don't think you're going to be considered an accessory to stroke."

"No," he said, shaking his head. "All I said was that a retirement community option was something that maybe we should talk about sometime. Which, in twenty-twenty hindsight, I shouldn't have."

She sat down in the blue plastic chair. "Have you always had such an incredibly well-honed sense of guilt?" she asked, watching him pace some more.

"The doctor here didn't say much of anything at all," he replied. "He just did some quick reflex tests, checked her eyes and her heart and then they rolled her out of here at a trot."

"Well, at least it wasn't at a gallop," Emily offered. "That would have been bad. Was Ida conscious for all this?"

He nodded. "She waved goodbye as they rolled her off for the CAT scan. She said something, but her speech is really slurred and I didn't understand a word of it."

"Has anyone given you an idea of how long the CAT scan is going to take?"

"No. No one's told me anything, Emily."

Ah, he was on the verge of slipping back into poor, pathetic and helpless again. "Well, I've got a bit of news for you."

He stopped in his tracks and stared at her. "You can't be pregnant. How could you know so soon?"

Good God, talk about absolutely illogical leaps. For a captain of industry, he sure didn't deal with the unexpected very well. Throw him one curve and his mind hooked on everything that came after it. "No, I'm not pregnant," she assured him. "But if anyone around here asks, I am your wife."

He didn't react. Not a blink, not a breath, not a swallow. Nothing.

"I had to tell them that so they'd let me in here," she explained. "Only immediate family is allowed. I suppose I could have told them I was just another grandchild, but that option didn't occur to me until just now."

He nodded. Very, very slightly, very, very slowly. "Thanks for being here."

"I came as soon as I heard that the ambulance run was for Ida. And I'll stay for as long as you need me."

"What about your roofing crew?"

"Amazingly enough, they said they'd done this sort of thing a few hundred times and that they didn't need any help from me. Go figure. I was crushed."

He smiled. Softly and genuinely. And it didn't flicker out in an instant, either. "You are incredible, Emily Raines."

"Yeah, I know," she replied. "You told me that last night. Twice as I recall."

"This is a different kind of incredible."

She was trying to decide if she wanted him to explain what he meant, when a tall, lean man wearing a pair of blue scrubs and carrying a metal clipboard, stepped into the doorway and knocked. Emily stood as she looked at the corners of his mouth for the telltale signs of bad news waiting to be told. And didn't see them. The guy was calm, relaxed, not at all worried. She locked her knees to keep from falling over as relief flooded through her.

"Mr. and Mrs. Preston?" he asked as he advanced into the exam room.

"Yes?" Cole replied for them.

"I'm Dr. Wilson, the neuro specialist on staff," he began, too busy looking at the chart on the clipboard to offer a handshake. "I've examined your grandmother and am going to admit her for twenty-four to forty-eight hours of observation."

"Observation?" Cole asked warily.

Dr. Wilson put the chart against his chest and crossed his arms over it. Rocking between his heels and toes, he replied, "The CAT scan shows that Mrs. Bentley has had what we call an ischemic stroke. Of the two kinds of stroke, it would be the one you'd pick to have if you got to choose. While the symptoms are shocking for everyone, usually because they're so sudden and unexpected, timely treatment of ischemic strokes can often prevent significant and permanent brain damage.

"We've administered the usual drugs to break up the arterial blockage and we should see a dramatic improvement in your grandmother's condition within the next twenty-four hours. We'll decide at that point about ongoing therapies and releasing her. Do you have any questions?"

Not any that he could answer at this point, Emily knew. In twenty-four hours, though... She hoped he wasn't one of those doctors who scheduled his rounds down to the millisecond.

"What room is she in?" Cole asked.

"Admitting will be able to tell you that in an hour or so. We like to give the nurses time to get the patients settled in before the family takes up camp."

He looked back and forth between them. "Why don't you two go get some lunch. By the time you get back, Mrs. Bentley will be in her room and ready to receive visitors. For a while anyway. It probably wouldn't be a good idea to tax her too much. She's had quite a day and she could use some rest."

He tapped the clipboard against the side of his leg, once, twice, said, "Well, I'll see you folks tomorrow," and walked out of the room.

"Thanks, Doc," Cole called after him.

Emily chimed in with a, "Yes, thank you," of her own and then stepped up to slip her arm around Cole's waist. "I don't know about you," she said, smiling up at him, "but good news always makes me hungry. Does anything sound good to you?"

"Are you sure it's good news?"

"I'm sure it could have been a whole, *whole* lot worse, Cole. Drugs and observation are about as light-weight as stroke interventions get."

"Okay," he said as she literally felt the tension drain out of him. He cocked a brow and smiled. "We were at a luau on a private beach when Grams woke me up."

Another one in the fantasy bag. But since it was his, she was going to let him surprise her. Right now, though… "I'm thinking a whole pig and pot of poi aren't going to be all that easy to find. But there is a kick-butt barbecue place a half block up the street. They have hot links and pulled-pork sandwiches. Will it do?"

"Anything will do," he admitted, taking her hand in his. "I just need to get out of here and pull myself together before we see Grams."

She grabbed her purse from the chair as he led her out the door. Cole Preston, man of steel nerves and laser focus, was on his way back. Letting him get his wits back on an even keel, she strode along at his side in silence as they left the hospital and made their way up the block to the Smoke Shack. They had their trays of food on the table in front of them before he spoke again.

"Do you think she's going to be all right, Emily?" he asked, sounding considerably stronger, more in charge, than he had even five minutes ago. "I mean, do you think that the drugs they've given her will undo all of the damage?"

She shrugged and continued cutting her sandwich in half. "No one knows until they know. Sometimes there's a miracle and there's no telling there was ever a stroke at all. Sometimes there's damage, but other parts of the brain compensate and there's pretty near normal functioning. And sometimes…"

"Sometimes what?" he asked, delaying her first bite.

"The consequences depend on what part of the brain was damaged and how severely. My grandmother had a stroke and physically you couldn't tell, but she lost her ability to make judgments about appropriate social behaviors."

"That's why she ran around naked?"

She took a bite of the brisket sandwich, nodded and then put it down on her plate. "Just so you know, Cole," she said, wiping the corners of her mouth with a paper napkin. "My nana lived a long and actually happy life after her stroke."

"Much happier than the people around her?"

She knew where he was going, what he was really asking. "There were days when, yes, she was the only one having a good time. But there were a lot more days that were really good for everyone."

They ate while he mulled all of that over. Her sandwich was history and she was down to her last few bites of coleslaw when he finally broke the silence.

"If you don't mind me asking, how did your grandmother die?"

He really did tend to dwell on the worst possibilities. "Nana walked into the front of a bus." The horrified look on his face was just what she'd been going for. "More accurately," she added, "she clipped the left front quarter panel of a city bus with the leg of her walker."

He chuckled silently and shook his head. "And the rest of the story?"

"She fell against the curb, broke her hip and went to a nursing home to heal and recover. For a while she did. And then she just slid away in a mental fog and her body eventually stopped. The term they use is clinical psychosis."

"That explains a lot, you know."

Yes, she did know. And maybe now that he knew,

too, it would make a difference in how he viewed the options for his grandmother. "There's usually a reason for the way people think about things," she allowed. "Reasons for what they do. People are far more rational and logical and deliberate than they often appear to be on the surface."

He leaned back in his seat and appeared to give that some thought, too. She watched as his gaze drifted off into his memories, saw the shimmer of tears form along the base of his lower lashes, heard him quietly clear his throat.

"Everything that I know about caring about people, about being a decent person, about being there when it counts, I owe to my grandmother," he said, reaching for his drink and blinking.

He took a quick sip and then went on. "When I was a kid, I spent all my summers and holidays with Grams. I never once heard her say a bad word about my mother or father. Not one, ever. But looking back as an adult, I can see that they were too busy with their own lives and ambitions and whatever to be parents. Grams picked up the slack.

"Every Thanksgiving, Christmas and Easter we served dinner at the homeless shelter. All those smelly, dirty, ratty… Most of them crazy… I can't tell you how many times I saw Grams sitting beside someone, her arm around their shoulder and looking at a tattered old picture they'd hauled out of their trash bag of belongings. Pictures of their moms, their kids, their war buddies, their beloved dog from childhood."

He laughed softly. "Pictures of people from magazines and newspapers they didn't really know but swore they did. She always took the time to listen and to care."

He sat forward to rest his forearms on the table. "She always carries a bunch of one-dollars bills, you know. The guy playing the sax in the subway, the bell ringer on the corner, the jars on the counters for a kid needing a kidney transplant. I think they've probably built at least a half dozen Ronald McDonald Houses with what she's put into the little collection boxes over the years. I guess, looking at it that way, pencils from an Indian Reservation aren't all that much different."

"Pencils?" she repeated.

"Three sets of address labels and a box of cedar number-two pencils came in today's mail. She sent the tribe money for vo-tech training. They sent her pencils as a thank-you."

"It's important to say thank you."

"And *please* and *may I?* and *excuse me* and *I'm sorry.* Grams has always been a stickler for the practice of good manners." He laughed again. "What I thought at the time had to be the worst spring break of any kid who had ever lived, I spent as a student at Miss Tanner's School of Social Graces. Day after day of which fork is for what, how to drink and eat, how to properly cut up anything that might show up on a plate. Sawing is done only by lumberjacks, you know."

"Well, I do now," she laughingly said.

"Good manners, Miss Tanner reminded us every morning, could ease the most awkward moment, open doors of opportunity that would otherwise be closed, and, if practiced with regularity, lead to a more civilized and peaceful world community."

He grinned and sighed. "Grams framed my certificate of completion. Next time you're over at her house, I'll show it to you. It's hanging on my bedroom wall. Right beside the door so that I see it and remember the lessons every time I walk out."

"And not just the ones Miss Tanner taught you. The lessons Ida has taught you, too."

His smile faded a bit, but didn't disappear completely. "You know what's really interesting? To me, anyway. I don't really have any strong childhood memories of times other than those I spent with Grams. The rest of it… It's all there, of course. I can remember people and places and things. It's just that in looking back at them, they don't mean very much."

Yeah, she could see how that would be. Ida was the one who raised him, the one who had given him all of her heart. It was perfectly understandable that she was in the center of his heart, his world, his life. It was just as understandable that her stroke had pulled the rug from under his feet.

Until today, the whole idea of Ida getting old and needing care was something that he hadn't really dealt with in any real, meaningful way. Instead of squaring up to the fact that Ida might someday be physically and mentally unable to care for herself, he'd put the whole solution thing into her needing to be protected from con artists and unscrupulous solicitors, from fraudulent contractors.

The day Cole Preston faced a world without his grandmother in it… He knew, deep down inside, the void he faced. And he was scared. It was that fear that lay under everything he did. The focus on business distracted him. The money he made, every cent of it, was earmarked for Ida's care, for buying the best medicine and any miracle he could find.

Ida was a very fortunate woman to be loved so deeply and completely. An ache bloomed in the center of Emily's chest and she felt her throat tightening with tears. Determined not to let emotion get the better of her, she picked up her drink, took a long pull through the straw and asked the first random question that popped into her mind.

"Was there ever a Gramps?"

Cole rolled his eyes and leaned slightly forward. "They eloped. He was killed in a tragic accident involving a third-story apartment, a grand piano and a frayed rope. In Chicago. Six months before my mother was born."

"Oh, that's too classic."

"Yeah, I've never believed it, either."

"Well," Emily offered in Ida's defense, "in those days there had to be a husband somewhere at some point, or you had to wear a big red *A* when you left the house. From what you've told me, I think that was probably the only concession to society's expectations that your grandmother has ever made in her life."

With a nod, he checked his watch. "They should have her settled in right about now. Are you ready to go back?"

Not that he really gave her much choice. "Anytime you are," she said, as he picked up her tray and carried it away.

As the nurse at the floor desk had told them, Grams was sound asleep. Cole watched Emily carefully smooth the blankets under his grandmother's arm and adjust the IV pole so that the line snaking into the back of her hand wasn't pulling at an odd angle. The little things Emily noticed, the kindnesses she so quietly and gently did…

"You look tired," he whispered as she came to stand beside him at the foot of the hospital bed.

"I am. A little," she whispered back.

"More like a *lot* tired. Why don't you kick back in the chair and catch a nap?"

She looked over at the huge green recliner that took up the corner of the room. "It's close to being a love seat." Looking up at him, she added, "Frankly, you look a little rough around the edges, too. We could share it and both catch a nap so that we're decent, cheerful company when Ida wakes up."

Hell, he was game for sharing anything with her. "This could be interesting," he observed, taking her hand and leading the way over to the corner.

"Yeah," she drawled as he dropped down into the chair, tipped the back and popped up the footrest. "Let's give your grandmother a heart attack on top of her stroke. I don't think so."

He held out his arms. Despite her protest, she didn't hesitate a second in climbing into the seat beside him. Turning on his side, he drew her into the curve of his body. She snuggled close, settled her head on the pillow of his arm and sighed in what sounded to him like utter contentment. He knew the feeling.

"Sweet Emily," he murmured, pressing a kiss into her golden curls. "You're—"

"If you say incredible, I'm going to buy myself a cape. With sequins."

He chuckled, his world suddenly so much brighter than he had imagined possible a few hours ago. "You're a very special person, Emily Raines. And I..." He swallowed hard and finished, "I'm thankful that you've come into my grandmother's life. Into my life."

She said something in reply, but sleep blurred the words into a soft purr.

Cole laid his cheek on her head and stared blankly out the window. It had been one helluva day, one helluva week, actually. Everything was turned upside down and inside out. His normal daily routine had been blown to smithereens. He was off his stride and not dealing very well with anything.

As soon as Grams was out of here and set up with all the caretakers and stuff she needed, he needed to get back to his regular life. And once he got his feet back under him and his world under control again... Then he could take a good look at his feelings, could decide if it was a matter of being caught up in the moment, or if he really did love Emily Raines.

And if he did... He closed his eyes, refusing to think about an entire lifetime of living upside down, inside out and out of control.

Eight

Cole held the front door open for Ida and her, sucking an audible breath through his teeth as his grandmother deliberately lifted her foot over the threshold. Emily understood exactly how nervous he felt; she had her hands up, prepared to catch Ida if the effort undid her balance and toppled her backward.

Ida managed to step back into her house without mishap, though, and Emily heard Cole sigh in relief in the same instant that she did.

"All right, you two," Ida firmly said, turning in the entryway to face them both. "We are going to come to an understanding right this minute."

"Wouldn't you like to sit down first?" her grandson suggested.

"Cole, dear," she replied crisply, "if I wanted to sit, I would. And I don't."

Cole was brave enough to mutter, "Okay," but Emily kept her mouth shut and tried to fade into the the grass cloth wallpaper. Man, she had never seen Ida the Queen before. Benevolent imperial command was the only way to describe the woman's approach. Well, okay. "Impressive" also worked.

"I have had a stroke, yes," she began, looking between them. "But as you clearly heard the doctor say as he was signing my discharge papers not more than an hour ago, I am a tough old buzzard. I am not in any way an invalid and I will not tolerate being treated as one. Is that clear?"

"Yes, ma'am," Cole said, sounding at least respectful if not exactly contrite.

"Emily?" Ida said, turning to her and making her heart jump. "Is that clear to you as well?"

Her stupid voice actually squeaked when she answered, "Yes, ma'am."

"Good." Ida turned and walked carefully into the living room, saying, "Now, I will sit down while we finish our conversation."

Cole followed her, pointing out, "Conversations usually involve more than one person talking, you know."

Ida, easing down in a wingback chair, countered, "You may talk all you like after I've gone into my office to write my thank-you notes." She tipped her head in the direction of the sofa and said quietly, but simply, "Sit."

They did as they were told, leaving the center cushion circumspectly between them.

"You both read the doctor's instruction sheet, did you not?"

They both nodded.

"And you are aware of the medications I'm to take? And how they are considered to be nothing short of miraculous in achieving positive results?"

They both nodded again.

"Good. Emily, has the barre been installed at the center yet?"

"The mirror wall went up yesterday morning," she explained. "The barre is supposed to go in this afternoon around three. At least that's what the installer promised me."

"Then I shall be there at four to begin my physical rehabilitation."

Cole shook his head. "I don't know, Grams. It—"

"Cole."

"Oh, God," he muttered, hanging his head.

"I understand that you and Emily have only the sincerest and best of intentions, but I do not need to be mothered and I will not tolerate being smothered. Independence is a fragile thing and it cannot survive coddling. I refuse to give mine up until my very last breath."

She looked back and forth between them and they dutifully replied in unison, "Yes, ma'am."

"Emily, my recollection is that you have slightly more than a week left until the grand opening celebration of the Augsburg Fine Arts Center. Am I correct?"

"Eight days."

"Don't you have a great deal to do in that time?"

Oh, damn. The queen was dismissing her. "Yes, I do."

"Then I suggest that your energies would be far better spent in seeing to the completion of your project than in hovering around me, waiting to catch me should I fall backward."

How had Ida known she'd done that?

"Cole," she said, turning attention to her grandson. "My understanding is that you have a business to run. Who has been minding it while you have been here visiting?"

He hesitated a moment and then finally answered, "There hasn't been much going on that's needed my input."

"Oh?" Ida said in what struck Emily as the epitome of a the-spider-said-to-the-fly tone. "Who called you this morning just before the doctor arrived for his final consultation?"

Oh, Cole was toast. Ida already knew the answer. They'd both known who was calling the second he'd answered his phone. The queen was setting up to dismiss her grandson, too.

"Jason."

"And what did your assistant have to say that required you to leave the room so your responses could not be overheard?"

He sighed and just looked at her.

"It is obviously time for you to go back to your life."

"Well, what if I don't want to?" he countered.

Ida slowly arched a silver brow. "If you think that resorting to the retort of a seven-year-old is appropriate, then it is most *definitely* time for you to be taking up your business activities again."

She looked between them again. "Thank you both for your loving attention the last twenty-four hours. I deeply appreciate and will forever treasure the depth of your concern for me. That having been said, please understand that I am returning the love and concern by my absolute insistence that you both go back to your respective lives. I will entertain no further discussion on the matter."

And with that pronouncement, she pushed herself to her feet with remarkable smoothness. "Now, if you will excuse me," she declared, walking out of the living room, "I have several dozen thank-you notes to write."

"Wow," Emily said in awe as Ida disappeared around the corner. "I've never seen this side of her before. Do you think that maybe the stroke has affected her personality?"

"Nope." He leaned back into the cushions and cradled the back of his head in his hands. "She actually took it easy on us. You should have been there the night the cops brought me home after catching me skinny-dipping in Central Park. I seriously thought about asking to be put into protective custody."

Emily smiled, but only until she saw his gaze. It was directed toward the ceiling, but focused on a distance far greater. She knew the look, knew what it meant. There was no point in pretending she didn't. No point in delaying the inevitable, either.

"So what did Jason have to say when he called

earlier?" she asked, trying very hard to sound way more casual than she felt.

"A congressional subcommittee is holding hearings on biofuels this week. The sugar cane lobby is scheduled to give their testimony on Thursday."

She supplied the next piece. "And they want to be able to tell Congress that they have the financial backing to be considered a serious player in the market."

"Yep. If they're taken seriously, then there will be government subsidies to fund further development."

"So you're basically the linchpin for their hopes."

He nodded, his gaze still far away. "If they're going to be ready to present the case they want to on Thursday, the deal needs to be done by tomorrow at the latest."

"It sounds to me," she quietly, "like you need to be headed for Louisiana tonight."

"They'd probably want me to appear with them before the subcommittee, too. Make the economic feasibility argument for them. And then make the pitch one-on-one during the weekend cocktail circuit."

It certainly sounded more glamorous than having a beer while sitting on the tailgate of a pickup truck in downtown Augsburg on a Saturday night. She couldn't blame him for being drawn to it. "Do you think C-SPAN will cover the hearings? I'd love to see you in action."

For the first time since Ida had left the room, his gaze came to hers. "You're assuming that I'm going to do all this."

"There's no assumption to it," she countered calmly. "I knew the second you walked back into the room after talking to Jason that a deal was on."

That seemed to take him aback. It only took him a second to recover, though. "Oh, yeah? How did you know that?"

"You were settled, centered, and I just knew. Ida knew it, too. She calls it your Hunter Look."

He considered her a moment as a myriad of emotions played across his features. She saw yearning and hunger, then doubt and regret. Resolve had slipped over his gaze when he reached for his phone. Her stomach tightened and rolled over, cold and heavy, as he flipped it open and hit the send button.

"Hey, Jase. What's the word from the flight crew?" he asked as she wondered how to extract herself from the situation with as much dignity as she could. "No way to fly around it or wait until it moves on through?"

She stood and looked at the door, wondering if maybe she should just make it easy on them both and walk out while he was still on the phone.

"Okay, I'm on my way," he promised his assistant. "Make the calls and get things ready to go. I'll meet you at the airport."

He flipped the phone closed and stood, saying, "There's a storm system moving in from the Gulf that's going to go stationary over the southeast for the next three days. I have a very small flying window to get in there before it does."

She nodded and put every bit of self-control she had

into a smile. "Then I'll wish you safe travels and smooth negotiations and get out of your way."

"Look, Emily," he said softly, kindly. "We've had a really good time, but—" His phone rang again and he snapped it open. "What, Jase?" He gritted his teeth. "Yes, forward it."

"Hang on a second," he instructed her, holding down the end button of his phone with his thumb. "I have to take—"

The phone rang and he instantly put it to his ear. "Hello, Mr. Brisbane. Yes, I am." There a very slight pause and then he walked over to his desk saying, "Yes, I had my assistant fax it here this morning. I've just come in the door and haven't had time to look at it. Okay, I have it right in front of me. I want Fontaine, Richards and Belleau there for sure. Tinley if he can make it on such short notice."

He was still talking, still organizing the players when she blew him a kiss he didn't see, and then left the house. She glanced back through the windshield of the Rover, hoping that the sound of the engine would at least bring him to the door to wave goodbye. It didn't.

"He's a money man," she told herself as she backed out of the drive and headed toward the warehouse. "And money men live to do the big-money deal. It's an addiction."

She managed to keep believing that was all it was until she closed her apartment door behind herself. The click of the latch echoed through her heart and filled her soul with an emptiness she had never known existed.

All the logic, all the rational pep talks about their relationship being a temporary fling, the caution she'd thought she'd exercised to keep her head squarely on her shoulders... Somehow, without her noticing, a hope for more, for love, had silently bloomed deep within her. Why the pain was ever so much deeper for not having realized that it had filled every corner of her heart until it died....

Tears welled in her eyes and spilled down her cheeks as she made her way blindly to her bed. Curling into a ball, her pillow clutched tightly to her heart, she sobbed for the loss of all that might have been.

"Another bourbon and Seven, Mr. Preston?"

He looked away from the window and up at Collete. "How many have I had already?"

"Two."

"I better call it quits," he admitted. "It's bad form to have the flight crew pour you down the steps when you land."

"Yes, it is. Would you care for something to eat now?"

The very thought of food made his stomach heave. He shook his head and looked back out the window.

He picked his cell phone up off the table, flipped it open and then stared at it as he sickeningly realized that he didn't have Emily's number in it. He'd never called her. Not once. She'd just been there whenever he'd wanted to find her. She'd come to him, without his having to ask, when she'd known that he needed her. She had become a daily, hourly part of his very existence and he'd never asked her for her phone number because it had never once crossed his mind that there would ever be a time that she wouldn't be an arm's length away.

He closed his eyes and mentally walked through Emily's apartment. No, no phone jack, no landline. With no four-one-one option, he scrolled through his contact list and found his grandmother's number. She picked up on the third ring.

"Hi, Grams. How are you doing?"

"I'm fine, Cole."

He took a steadying breath. "Did you get down to Emily's to work on the barre this afternoon?"

"I did. It's absolutely lovely. Emily does things with such panache, such… Well, in the popular vernacular, class."

Yeah, God knew she had way more class than he did. "How did your exercise session go?" he asked. "You didn't push yourself too far, did you?"

"Not at all. I know that I am not in dancing condition. I know how to pace myself."

He drew another deep breath. "Was Emily there to help you?"

"I allowed her to hover nearby to relieve her anxiety. But I didn't need any help, Cole."

"Of course," he said, wincing. Out of options, he bit the bullet. "You wouldn't happen to have her phone number, would you?"

"No. I've never needed it. If I want to talk to Emily, I simply go find her."

"Well, Grams, I can't quite do that at forty thousand feet over Louisiana." He hadn't meant to let his frustration show, but it was there, resonating in the air and demanding that his next words be an apology.

His grandmother cut off his attempt to spit one out by saying sweetly, "Well, Cole, dear… Again in the popular vernacular, it certainly sucks to be you."

"Grams!" he said, not sure whether he was more stunned or appalled.

"I would suggest that if talking to Emily by telephone were truly important to you, you would have seen that you asked her for her number before you left."

Okay, so much for being cool; desperate was desperate. "Could you ask her what it is and call me with it?"

"No. I did my part in bringing you and Emily together. You are responsible for what you ultimately do with the possibilities. Now, I hate to cut this conversation short, Cole, but *Dancing with the Stars* is coming on and I never miss it."

She was done and he knew that there was no hope of getting her to change her mind. "Good night, Grams."

"Good luck."

He flipped the phone closed and stared across the cabin, his mind numb, but not nearly numb enough. Grams had set him up. Deliberately. The whole thing about liquidating part of her investment portfolio to give the money to Emily had been a ruse. A ruse designed to get him to Augsburg and keep him there long enough for him to be…seduced. Seduced by Emily Raines!

No. He wasn't being fair. Emily had been just as much a victim of his grandmother's matchmaking as he was. He was absolutely sure of it. He'd bet the damned plane on it.

And, as long as he was engaged in an honest analysis, the truth was that neither one of them could claim that the other had seduced them. It had been mutual from the first moment. Every second had been exhilarating. Every second the stuff, literally, of his fantasies. He'd never been so happily oblivious to the rest of the world, or felt so utterly…loved.

He closed his eyes as the fullness of reality settled into his brain. His grandmother had set him up. Set him up to be seduced by the loving heart of Emily Raines.

And what had he done with such a wondrous, precious, undeserved gift? He'd put his world back on an even keel. He'd put his business ahead of Emily. He'd tucked his tail and run away.

There were no words to describe what a fool he was, what a coward he was and how badly he'd blown it.

Nine

Emily stepped back to get a better perspective of her handiwork. Work, yes, handy, no, she admitted as she considered how the *G* in *Grand* was a good three inches smaller that the *O* in *Opening,* and how all the letters in her sign went slightly uphill to the right. Well, add another thing to the long list of things she had bungled, screwed up, forgotten or just outright mangled in the last two days. Too used to failing to be disgusted anymore, she tossed her paintbrush in the water can and sat down on one of the empty wire spools the electricians had been kind enough to leave behind.

Maybe the fourth attempt at a front window banner would be the charm. Or not. She'd decide how she felt about trying tomorrow. Tomorrow might be the day when she woke up feeling rested and her brain would function right instead of four beats behind. That would help considerably.

"Where would you like these machines unloaded, ma'am?"

She looked over her shoulder. A man in a gray work uniform stood in the opening of the warehouse delivery bay. One label on his shirt front said George. The other one said National Freight. He held a clipboard stuffed with paper in his hand.

"What machines?" she asked, pushing herself to her feet.

"Well, let's take a quick look-see," he replied, leafing through the papers. "I got on board some lathes, planers, joiners, table saws, drill presses and what looks like more hand and power tools than Carter's got pills."

He squeezed the clamp and pulled the papers free. "Here's the bill of lading," he explained as he handed them to her. "I need your signature down there at the bottom where the red *x* is."

She had taken a pen from him, too, before what he was saying really registered. "I'm sorry, but there's been some sort of mistake. I didn't order these things. I don't have the money to pay for them. I wish I did, but I don't."

"The receipt's on the bottom of the stack there," George said. "I probably should have put it on the top for you. Sorry about that."

She pulled it out. Her name and address were in the delivery box. Other than that… She ran her gaze down the column of numbers to the total at the bottom. The amount was so staggeringly huge that even her befuddled brain wrapped instantly around it.

"Who bought all of this?" she asked, quickly turning the receipt over to see if there was anything on the back. There wasn't.

"I don't know, ma'am. They hand me the papers, give me an address and a map, and send me out. I don't need to know any more than that to do my job."

God, it was nice to have her brain back. She'd really missed it. "I don't know about this. I really think a mistake has been made," Emily persisted. "Can you hold off unloading for a few minutes and let me call the store?"

"Sure."

Heading for the office at the front of the building, thankful that Beth had reminded her to hook her cell phone up to the charger that morning, Emily looked down at the total for the machinery and tools again. Lord Almighty.

Ida was sitting on the office chair, changing into her dance shoes when Emily reached the office.

"Is there a problem, dear?" she asked as Emily found and unplugged her phone.

"There's a huge truck out back loaded high and tight with brand-new shop machinery and tools that the driver tells me someone bought for me," she explained as she carefully punched in the store's phone number and hit the send button.

"Perhaps your Secret Santa decided that you deserve more than he gave you."

"My Santa deals in cash."

The phone at the Home Center rang once and the automated system picked up. She was waiting to be told what number to push for customer service when Beth threw open the front door, grabbed the doorjamb and breathlessly exclaimed, "Emily! There's a kitchen design truck on the north side of the building and they want to know which door would be best to bring the stuff in through. Where did you get the money for a mega industrial be-still-my-heart all stainless steel kitchen?"

Aw, Jesus. "I didn't buy a kitchen," Emily assured her friend, snapping the phone closed and heading out the door. "I didn't buy shop machines and tools, either."

"Tools?" Beth asked as she blew past her.

The truck was right where Beth had said it was. This delivery man was wearing a blue uniform. His name was Edmond and he worked for Exclusive Kitchens and More. She'd heard of them. Upscale, high dollar, Kansas City.

She came to a halt in front of him and didn't even bother to ask questions. "Sir, I'm afraid that someone has gone way out of control in the practical joke department. I didn't order a kitchen. Right now, I'd have to take out a loan to buy a George Foreman Grill at Wally World. I'm sorry you drove all the way down here, but you're just going to have to haul it all back."

He stood there looking at her, probably waiting to see if she was really done with her rant. Either that or he was trying to decide if he could make it to the cab of his truck before she went totally berserk and attacked him.

"It's paid for, too, Emily."

From behind her. Cool, controlled, calm. Cole. Her heart swelled and her knees went weak. Drawing what she could of a breath, Emily lifted her chin and slowly turned, hoping that he wouldn't notice how her pulse was racing.

He stood just outside the front door, his hands in the pockets of his khakis, his dark hair, as always, just brushing the collar of his shirt. The wary hope in his eyes as he met her gaze… Her traitorous heart skittered and danced.

"You bought all of this stuff," she said. A statement of the obvious. An acknowledgment of an action taken. Nothing more. She couldn't give him any more of herself than she already had.

"Show them where you want the kitchen installed," he said easily. "And tell the guy out back where you want the equipment placed. Then let's talk."

God, she didn't want to talk. She didn't want to think. She wanted him to wrap her in his arms, hold her close and hear him say that he loved her with all of his heart. Not that that was the way their exchange was likely to go. The idea of having an audience watching her struggle to keep her composure…

"My apartment," she said quietly as she walked past him. "In twenty minutes."

Cole watched her march off with her shoulders squared, her hands fisted, and fought the urge to go after her, to throw his arms around her and beg her to forgive him, to beg her to let him back into her heart. It ached clear to the center of his soul to know that he'd so badly hurt her, that he'd been so incredibly stupid and selfish. He wanted things right between them, right now. He wanted to be whole again.

But that decision was Emily's to make and he had no choice but to allow her to make it on her terms, in her time. He expelled a long, hard breath, then tipped his face up to the warmth of the spring sunshine and deliberately tried to push the fear away long enough to figure out what he was going to say and how he was going to say it when the twenty minutes were up and the rest of his life was on the line.

It took her thirty minutes. Five to show George where the wood shop was, ten to turn Edmond over to Beth and fifteen to get her heart swallowed down and her hands to quit trembling.

Rising from the arm of the sofa as she came through the door, he turned to face her. He started to speak, but she cut him off, saying breezily, "I thought you were supposed to be in Washington today," as she headed into the kitchen on the pretense of getting a soft drink from the fridge. Anything to avoid having to face him square on and look him in the eye. Anything to keep him from seeing how broken her heart was without him.

"They can handle it without me. I have more important things to do."

She desperately wanted to hear him say that she was the most important thing to him, but since he hadn't…

"And playing Santa is more important to you than testifying before Congress?"

"Grams is today's Secret Santa, Emily," he informed her quietly. "Not me. All I did was sell some of her stock to cover the cost."

Oh. God. What he'd wrongly suspected at the very beginning. And she'd thought that the mess of their relationship couldn't get any worse. "I never asked her to do that," Emily protested, her pulse racing. "I didn't ask her to do—"

"I know," he said, gently but firmly cutting her off. "I know a lot of things today that I didn't know two days ago when I left here. Grams set us both up. She admitted that the whole I-want-to-give-Emily-money thing was a ruse. She knew that I'd drop everything and make a beeline for Augsburg to shut down her big donation effort *du jour.*"

"Which is exactly what you did."

"I'm nothing if not predictable, huh?" he offered with a wry smile and quick shrug of one shoulder. "Grams wanted us to meet and she figured that was the quickest and most efficient way to get it done. And it worked just as she'd planned."

"Ida the matchmaker," Emily said, turning over in her mind all of Ida's comments, all the looks, all the questions. Now that it had been put out in the open… Damn it all, she should have seen what her friend was up to right from the beginning. She could have saved herself so much pain if she'd only known and nipped it in the bud.

He nodded. "I had no idea she was so good at it."

"Well," Emily allowed, thinking she could at least try

to be gracious, "she gets points for recognizing the potential for good sexual chemistry, anyway. That part was really good. Beyond that..."

Emily dragged a deep breath into her lungs and willed her stupid knees to quit shaking. "So, if the suggestion of giving me a big donation was a ruse to get you here, to get us to meet, why did you sell her stocks? Why did you allow it to go from a ruse to reality?"

"Because she wanted to do it and it would have been wrong for me to stand in the way."

Well, there was an unexpected answer. Were there more of them? Could she really hope that this wasn't going to end with a cordial, mature adult handshake and an empty promise to keep in touch?

Her heart thundering and her mouth suddenly dry, she popped the top on her soda can and took a big sip. It didn't really help all that much, but it did at least give her a chance to put a coherent thought together that didn't sound totally desperate.

"You seem," she ventured, "to have had a considerable change in your thinking on the matter in the last forty-eight hours or so."

Finally. Thank God, they were finally to the beginning of what needed to be said. Cole tamped down the urge to walk around the kitchen counter and dispense with all the damn talking. Instead, he nodded slowly and confessed, "I've done a lot of thinking in the last few days, Emily. And one of the subjects I've given a bit of thought to is Grams and her charitable tendencies. You're right. Absolutely, one hundred and ten percent right. It's her money and if she wants to use it to make the world a better place, I don't have any right to stand in her way."

"Just how extensive is this newfound acceptance of yours? Does it go all the way to the funding of the whale-speak dictionary? Or does it go just far enough to cover a commercial kitchen and woodworking machinery for me?"

"I've done some real stupid things lately," he freely admitted, "but I do know better than to try to buy my way back into your good graces."

She gave him a small smile in reward for his honesty and then asked, "So now that you've seen that all of Ida's gifts have been delivered... What's next? Are you heading for Washington now?"

"No."

"I thought they really wanted you there to help present their project to congress."

"Plain and simple, Emily," he answered on the courage of his heart's desire. "I don't want to be there. I want to be here. With you."

With you. Her heart swelled and her soul danced. Her mind sadly warned that she was grasping for a hope that might not really be there. She put the soda can on the counter so he couldn't see how badly her hands were suddenly shaking.

It took everything she had to keep her voice from cracking as she asked, "How long are you planning to be here this time?"

"That's up to you."

Yes, it was. And she needed to draw the line so he knew precisely where it was. And as painful as it might turn out to be, she needed to draw it now so that she didn't hope for more than he would ever be willing and able to give her.

"Cole," she said, coming around the counter to stand in front of him. "I've discovered that I don't like being a disposable person. It hurts. Deeply."

He nodded as though he actually understood, then reached up to slowly trail a fingertip over her lips and whisper, "What would I have to do to get you to give me a second chance?"

A second chance at what? her mind wondered even as her heart said that it didn't matter. He was here and they were together. There were no guarantees in love.

"A second chance to get it right, Emily," Cole murmured, gently taking her face between his hands. She looked up at him and he saw the depth of his own hope in her searching gaze.

"I've never felt emptier or more alone than I have the last two days," he offered, pouring the desperation of his heart into each and every word. "I've turned to talk to you a thousand times and you weren't there. I've reached out to touch you and you weren't there. All the business, all the wheeling and dealing… I have no idea what I signed, Emily. I just put my name on the paper so that it was done and I could come home to you.

"I don't want to spend the rest of my life missing you. The ache is horrible and forever deep. Please, Emily. Please give me another chance. Let me prove, every single day for the rest of our lives, how much I love you."

Her heart brimming, Emily smiled up at him. "I love you with all that I am, Cole," she promised.

The relief flooding his soul nearly buckled his knees. Cole wrapped his arms around her and drew her close, holding her tight, letting her fill him with the strength of her endless love and the sweet, absolute certainty that his heart and soul had indeed come home.

* * * * *

Don't miss the next book in
GIFTS FROM A BILLIONAIRE.
Look for THE MAGNATE'S TAKEOVER
by Mary McBride,
available this November
from Silhouette Desire.

Well, it wasn't the first time he'd encountered a pretty woman who'd had too much to drink, David Halstrom thought, but it was certainly the first time he'd witnessed a woman four feet off the ground clinging to a lamppost or one who looked like an inebriated fallen angel. She was so damn pretty, even in the dim lamplight, with her strawberry blond hair and her spattering of freckles, that he'd almost forgotten why he'd come to this derelict hellhole in the first place.

He sighed and supposed he ought to check on her so he walked in the direction of the buzzing, nearly burned-out vacancy sign. He knocked on the door, waited a moment, and when nobody answered, he entered what appeared to be the office of this dump that she claimed to manage.

The office was as tawdry as he expected, like something right out of the fifties if not earlier. It didn't surprise him a bit to see a small black-and-white television with foil-wrapped rabbit ears wedged into a corner of the room, right next to a windowsill lined with half-dead plants. Good God. Did people actually stay here? Did they *pay* to stay here?

He knocked softly on a nearby door, then he opened it a few inches and saw a dimly lit bedroom that wasn't quite as tattered as the lobby. There was a faint odor of lavender in the little room, and in the center of the bed, beneath the covers, he recognized an angel-sized lump.

Good, he thought. She'd sleep it off and tomorrow she'd have a headache to remind her that cheap wine had its perils.

"Sleep well, angel," he whispered. "When you lose this job, you can come to work for me."

He quietly closed the door and returned to the parking lot.

A quick walk around the dismal property only served to confirm all of David's suspicions. The place was a total wreck in dire need of demolition, which he would be more than happy to arrange. He got back in his car and headed for his hotel on the other side of the highway. As he drove, his thumb punched in his assistant's number on his cell phone.

Jeff Montgomery was probably in the middle of dinner, he thought, but the call wouldn't surprise him, nor would David's demand for instant action. The man had worked for him for five years and seemed to thrive on the stress and the frequent travel as well as the variety of tasks that David tossed his way, from *Make sure my tux is ready by six* to *Put together a proposal for that acreage in New Mexico.*

This evening David told him, "I need to know everything there is to know about the Haven View Motor Court across from the hotel. Who owns it? Is there any debt? What's the tax situation? Everything. And while you're at it, see what you can dig up on a woman named Libby Jost. Have it on my desk tomorrow morning, Jeff. Ten at the latest."

"You got it, boss," came the instant reply. David Halstrom was used to instant replies.

He was used to getting precisely what he wanted, in fact, and he figured he'd own the ramshackle Haven View Motor Court lock, stock, and barrel in a few days, or a week at the very most. And if he didn't exactly own the fallen strawberry blond angel by then, at least she'd be on his payroll.

* * * * *

Her breath whistled out in a sigh of relief when he exited Customs. Devon recognized him right away from the newspaper and magazine articles her friend and partner Sabrina had looked up during her frantic prep work.

Caleb John Logan, Jr. Thirty-one. Six-two. With jet-black hair, laser-blue eyes and a linebacker's shoulders under his charcoal-gray cashmere overcoat. His jaw-dropping good looks didn't score him any points with Devon. She'd learned the hard way not to trust handsome heartbreakers like Cal Logan.

But he was a client. An important one. And she was willing to give someone who'd served a hitch in the marines before earning a B.S. from the University of

Oregon, an MBA from Stanford and his first million at the ripe old age of twenty-six the benefit of the doubt.

Right up until he spotted the hot-pink pashmina, that is.

Devon knew the flash of color was more visible than the sign she held up with his name on it. So she wasn't surprised when Logan picked her out of the crowd and cut in her direction. She'd just plastered on her best businesswoman smile when he whipped an arm around her waist. The next moment she was sprawled against his cashmere-covered chest.

"Hello, brown eyes."

Swooping down, he covered her mouth with his.

Sheer astonishment kept Devon rooted to the spot for a few seconds while her mind whirled chaotically. Her first thought was that her client had downed a few too many drinks during the long flight. Her second, that he'd mistaken the kind of escort and consulting services her company provided. Her third shoved everything else out of her head.

The man could kiss!

His mouth moved over hers with a skill that ignited sparks at a half dozen flash points throughout her body. Devon hadn't experienced that kind of spontaneous combustion in a while. A *long* while.

The sparks were still popping when she pushed off his chest, only now they fueled a flush of anger.

"Do you always greet women you don't know with a lip-lock, Mr. Logan?"

A smile crinkled the skin at the corners of his eyes. "As a matter of fact, I don't. That was from Don."

"Huh?"

"He said he owed you one from New Year's Eve two years ago and made me promise to deliver it."

She stared up at him in total incomprehension. Logan hooked a brow and attempted to prompt a non-existent memory.

"He abandoned you at the Waldorf. Five minutes before midnight. To deliver twins."

"I don't have a clue who or what you're…"

Understanding burst like a water balloon.

"Wait a sec. Are you talking about Sabrina's old boyfriend? Your buddy, who's now an ob-gyn doc?"

It was Logan's turn to look startled. He recovered faster than Devon had, though. His smile widened into a rueful grin.

"I take it you're not Sabrina Russo."

"No, Mr. Logan, I am *not*."

* * * * *

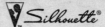

MARRIED BY CHRISTMAS

Playboy billionaire Elijah Vanaldi has discovered he is guardian to his small orphaned nephew. But his reputation makes some people question his ability to be a father. He knows he must fight to protect the child, and he'll do anything it takes. Ainslie Farrell is jobless, homeless and desperate—and when Elijah offers her a position in his household she simply can't refuse....

Available in November

HIRED: THE ITALIAN'S CONVENIENT MISTRESS

by

CAROL MARINELLI

Book #29